Dedalus Africa
General Editors: Jethro Sou␟
                 Yovanka Perdigão

Saara

MBAREK OULD BEYROUK

SAARA

translated by
Rachael McGill

Dedalus

This book has been selected to receive financial assistance from English PEN's "PEN translates" programme, supported by Arts Council England. English PEN exists to promote literature and our understanding of it, to uphold writers' freedoms around the world, to campaign against the persecution and imprisonment of writers for stating their views, and to promote the friendly co-operation of writers and the exchange of ideas.

Published in the UK by Dedalus Limited
24-26, St Judith's Lane, Sawtry, Cambs, PE28 5XE
info@dedalusbooks.com
www.dedalusbooks.com

ISBN printed book 978 1 915568 68 7
ISBN ebook   978 1 915568 71 7

Dedalus is distributed in the USA & Canada by SCB Distributors
15608 South New Century Drive, Gardena, CA 90248
info@scbdistributors.com   www.scbdistributors.com

Dedalus is distributed in Australia by Peribo Pty Ltd
58, Beaumont Road, Mount Kuring-gai, N.S.W. 2080
info@peribo.com.au   www.peribo.com.au

First published by Dedalus in 2025
Saara copyright © Editions Elyzad 2022 by arrangement of Florence Giry Agency (FGA) Paris
Translation copyright © Rachael McGill 2025

Printed and bound in the UK by Clays Elcograf S.p.A.
Typeset by Marie Lane

THE AUTHOR

Mbarek Ould Beyrouk (Beyrouk) was born in Atar, Mauritania, in 1957. A journalist, he founded the country's first ever independent newspaper, Mauritanie Demain, in 1988, and is a recognised champion of free speech. He was honoured for his media work in 2006 through an appointment to the Higher Authority for the Printed and Audiovisual Press in Mauritania, and he is currently an advisor to the President of the Republic.

He has written seven novels: *Et le ciel a oublié de pleuvoir* (2006), *Le griot de l'émir* (2013), *Le tambour des larmes* (*The Desert and the Drum*) (2015) *Je suis seul* (2018), *Parias* (2021), *Le silence des horizons* (2021) and *Saara* (2022).

THE TRANSLATOR

Rachael McGill is a playwright for stage and radio, prose writer and translator of novels and plays from French, German, Spanish and Portuguese. Her short stories have been published in several anthologies and online. She has translated three books for Dedalus: *The Desert and the Drum* and *Saara* by Mbarek Ould Beyrouk and *Co-wives, Co-widows* by Adrienne Yabouza.

Her translations of *The Desert and the Drum* and *Co-wives, Co-widows* were both shortlisted for The Oxford-Weidenfeld Translation Prize and her translation of Kerstin Specht's play *Marieluise* won the Gate Theatre/Allied Domecq translation prize.

Her first novel *Fair Trade Heroin* was published by Dedalus in 2022.

SAARA

MBAREK OULD BEYROUK

translated by Rachael McGill

SAARA

The city seemed to have lost its way; the population blind and bewildered, the roads no longer certain where they led. Life had a new rhythm, in which people walked with their heads bowed, talked without looking at each other, struggled to name unnameable things. They'd say, 'Nothing's like it was before,' without being able to explain what they meant by 'nothing' or 'before'. They tried to distract themselves with pastimes, pleasures, prayers, but they couldn't stop glancing towards the mountain. Up there, they knew, outlandish things were happening.

I'd always thought I was different, but I was plagued by the same unease. Part of me longed to escape, to flee to some crass megalopolis like my sister had. It wasn't that I believed the nonsense about the mountain being possessed by *jinns*, the spectres of the night. I knew my disquiet came from inside me.

I worried that happiness was slipping from my grasp; that all that surrounded me—stones, wind, sky, sun, moon and stars—was preparing to enter a period of mourning. I worried that the faces of those I loved were fading from my mind; that soon I'd have nothing but memories and fleeting encounters. My hands, it seemed, had forgotten how to grasp happiness. My heart could no longer be stirred.

I knew no remedy for such pain, so I tried to ignore it. I told myself the future might bring brighter things. I walked down the street as before; smiling at people, kissing acquaintances, spouting silly nonsense at the top of my voice. I cultivated nonchalance, but it was impossible not to notice the silences. Fear crouched behind people's eyes, caught in their throats when they tried to speak. Heads turned incessantly towards the mountain, ears listened out for the cries. I turned my own head in the other direction.

They said the spectre that lived up there and emitted those monstrous cries was very powerful, that the *jinns* of a new era were starting to surround us, threatening our way of life: our loves, our beliefs, our fields, our water, even our prayers. Soon the *jinns* would come down from the high peaks and flood into our valley. No one dared walk the stony paths that led out of the city. They said animals that ventured up there never returned, that the wells had dried up, the trees were stunted and creaked with pain, the lizards had grown giant, that the jackals had sprouted wings and pointed teeth, even that the raindrops that fell so rarely up there were as salty as tears.

I knew this communal terror to be the senseless chatter of primitive brains. Because we couldn't explain our troubles—the sky that forgot to rain, the ever more frequent sandstorms, the dried up oases, the children born deformed, even the soaring prices—we attributed them to monsters, to alien forces, to the mountain.

Still, the city of Atar no longer felt like home. My love for the place hadn't changed; it was more that something inside me had withered. Perhaps I'd just exhausted my ability to stifle my sadness.

There was a time when I'd vowed to tear down the walls that separated me from my dreams. I did have dreams. But they got buried beneath lies, betrayals, false smiles and beautiful, smooth bodies. Once the hope in me was crushed, I decided to dedicate myself to sensation-seeking, to the pleasures of the flesh. I embraced the moment, savoured those ephemeral joys that ignite with one breath and go out again with the next. A nice word for me would be courtesan. Another word might be slut. As a rule, though, I did choose my lovers.

To return to the fears of the people of my town: perhaps they were felt so deeply because we had no way of measuring the weight of the burden we carried. We couldn't see what was ahead of us: the mountain concealed whatever horrors were lurking at its peaks. It sat there: calm, placid, imposing, silent. In the mornings, it wore its brightest colours; in the afternoons, it draped itself in soft, burnished robes. There were no signs of torment written on its stones. Yet at nightfall we did hear screams. There was something deeper at the root of our anxiety too; something I wasn't sure I understood. I determined to clear my mind of negative thoughts, to get on with life.

That was harder to do than before. People were hiding away, behind closed doors and prejudice. The men no longer fooled around in public; the stares in the street were getting nastier; those spiteful women, the kind who concealed their feelings and their failures behind sharp words, were raising their voices louder. Everywhere, doors were banging shut. But that wasn't what was blocking me.

No, I knew where I was going, or at least I thought I did. I'd wriggled free years ago of their rules, their wagging fingers. Freedom had chosen me, but it had enslaved me too: I had no father, no mother, no gossiping cousins. I was left alone when I was very young, and that solitude had shaped me: assembled me, disassembled me, melted me down.

My mother left first. I was five years old. She turned her back on a violent husband and two daughters who, if the neighbours were to be believed, she loved very much. Probably she told herself the shouting and insults were no longer bearable, that marriage should not mean violence, that it was better to leave your loved ones than to wake up every day crying. I never believed the story that one old neighbour, Emma, always told. She said that on the day she left, my mother addressed the whole neighbourhood, saying, 'I can't look at his face any more; I loathe him. I reject everything to do with him, even our daughters. I don't want them any more, little girls born from rape who look like him. I can't bear to see anything that reminds me of the person I hate!' I was sure she hadn't said anything like that, but there was no denying she'd abandoned us. I couldn't remember much about her face, only that she had a scar on her forehead. It was very visible, but it didn't make her ugly. I also remembered the last night she spent with us: the crying in the bedroom, her screams, her running into the street half-naked, wailing, the

neighbours crowding around her. That was the last time I saw
her. She left under the protection of the neighbours. The next
day, they made my father agree before the *qadi* to a divorce.

My sister and I stayed with him. He didn't hit us at first,
but he terrified us. Whenever he looked at us, we trembled
and couldn't speak. He addressed us in growls, repeated that
our mother was filth and that we took after her. We left the
house only to go to school, and sometimes he would follow us
there, to make sure we didn't stray. Then came his new wives.
They didn't like us, because our father showed no interest
in us, except for one, whose name was Samia. She was very
young. She taught us how to do our hair, to put on make-up,
even to smile. She also taught us beautiful songs, and stood up
for us when our father scolded us. But one day he raised his
hand to her and she left. We heard them exchanging insults
and blows through the night, Samia screaming, 'How dare you
hit me? You're a monster and you always will be! Even your
daughters, your own daughters, so pretty and nice…' The rest
was lost in the din. The next morning at dawn, she slammed
the door and we never saw her again.

After that, our father became angrier and more violent.
We put up with his hysterical rages and the occasional slap,
but then he started really hitting us. We grew up quickly
then. I felt I was becoming a woman, and I realised I was no
longer prepared to put up with his constant aggression. I'd had
enough of living in fear, and I couldn't stand to see him touch
my little sister. One day, when he rushed towards her for some
mundane reason, I got between them and pushed him away
as hard as I could. I didn't realise my own strength: he hit the
door frame and lost consciousness. My sister screamed, but

I didn't panic. I poured some water on his face. He opened his eyes and was shocked, I think, by what he saw: his eldest daughter with a look of defiance on her face, determined not to accept his tyranny.

I think his spirit was broken that day. He stopped opening the shop that adjoined our house, stopped going to the fields to pick mint and alfalfa. He sank into a kind of lethargy from which he never recovered. After a while he stopped speaking, then he stopped moving. We felt like orphans again, and soon we were: our father faded away soundlessly one morning, while I was trying to get him to drink some milk. I thought I saw a kind of plea in his eyes as they dimmed. I was able to tell him before he left us that we forgave him. In that moment, it seemed to me that he died happy.

We took charge. Rummaging around the house, I found a small stash of money. I decided to re-open the shop. I bought some stock from Ahmedou, the market wholesaler, just to cover the basic needs of people in our modest neighbourhood: tea, sugar, rice, sweets. In imitation of all good shopkeepers, I wrote the customary phrase above the door: 'Credit is dead, peace and salvation to its soul.' My sister found work as a cleaner at a guest house on the edge of town: she got up very early and didn't get home until late. There was no rush of customers to my little shop, and I spent most of my time sitting behind the counter, chatting to the local girls. I discovered that men liked me: they often lingered while they shopped; some gave me compliments; some even wrote me poems. It made me smile, but it didn't turn my head.

My sister and I led a quiet life. We were poor, but we usually had the essentials. Everything was going all right, or so I thought: we were almost happy—a little lonely, perhaps, but free of our torments, united and strong. Our mother's absence didn't weigh too heavily on us. We didn't know what had become of her, and we no longer wanted to know. We told ourselves every night that if she really loved us, she'd have come back when our father died. Perhaps she had a new family, new children, now.

We had no fears. The people in the neighbourhood protected us, and praised us for being sensible and brave. At night, we slept peacefully, snuggled together. Then, one evening, when I'd kept the shop open late, the spectre came upon me that would stay with me forever. The door of the shop was slammed shut. I didn't have time to scream: then confusion, fear, pain, my skin violated, rawness, the feeling of being ripped apart, my limbs scattered to the four corners, my skin stretched taut, hands choking me, others digging into me, my clothes in tatters, swords tearing at me, and the fear, the sense of contamination, of absolute abandonment, of terrible, painful solitude, that the world had delivered me to the clutches of something unspeakable. I died, and it was a shameful end: I was forced to watch what should have belonged to me alone dying inside me. I dragged myself home and wept silently all night. The next day, I didn't know how to voice my pain, so I kept it to myself. I even hid it from my sister. I couldn't tell the world that I'd become worthless, been brought low by thugs. I couldn't prove it either. My attackers were well-brought up boys from some of the most respected families in town, whereas I… they'd just deny it, they'd find witnesses, I'd look like a spiteful girl trying to blackmail some rich kids. Who would dare take my side?

SaaRa

Our little shop remained closed for several days, then I sold off all the stock at a loss. Not long after that, my little sister left. She gave me no warning. I got a note one day from the owner of the guest house where she worked, saying, 'I've met the man of my dreams. We've left together. Don't be angry. I love you.' Apparently I was not her sister for life. I'd never turned away from her when she had a fever, never slept without feeling her by my side. I'd faced our father, the terror of our childhoods, for her, sacrificed myself for her, slept on an empty stomach so she could eat her fill. None of that mattered. I was appalled by her desertion, felt betrayed, yet I never stopped thinking about her for a second. She'd left for love, but hadn't I given her that? Could more than one love not co-exist?

To stop myself going crazy, all alone in a house that was now too big, I invited an elderly relative with no children to come and live with me. I also started spending time with Mina. She was older than me, always smiling, open and funny. I started going to her place in the evenings, trying to escape my boredom and distress. An endless stream of young people passed through Mina's home; there were tea parties, music performances, dances, polite conversations and some that were more risqué. Suggestive glances were exchanged, poems were composed and recited. I was amazed to discover a whole side of life that had nothing to do with struggle, drudgery, abandonment, violence, or loss. Mina watched over me like an elder sister. She also sent me on errands—to buy bread or sweets, to pick up take-away food—and often asked me to make the tea. Sometimes she seemed to forget I wasn't her maid, but I was happy to soak up the joyful atmosphere, to be surrounded by a zest for life I'd never known possible. Gradually, I learned a new language. It was made up of innuendo, irony, subtle suggestions that added nothing to the meanings of words but cloaked them in beautiful intrigue. I was filled with wonder at the new society I'd entered. I learned to apply my make-up, to dress and to speak just like the 'better-bred people'.

One day, as I was about to go out, I found Hamza on my doorstep. Hamza was a close friend of Mina's; a lover, perhaps, I wasn't sure. He came from a rich family, was what people called 'a good catch'. He wasn't exactly handsome, but he was elegant and witty. I couldn't decide whether I should invite him in, or whether that would be unacceptable. I asked him, shakily, 'What are you doing here, Hamza?'

I sensed I'd used the wrong words, had sounded suspicious. That was no way to welcome a visitor. It struck me that perhaps Mina just wanted to see me and had sent Hamza to fetch me. But he spared no time in declaring his love for me. He said he'd been dreaming about me; that he wanted to love me, protect me, serve me, even marry me. While I was still reeling at this, he kissed me. Something flooded into me and froze my body and mind. I was unable to move to push him away. When I'd recovered my senses, I set off running towards Mina's house, as if seeking her protection. Hamza came after me. When we arrived there together, I saw the surprise on my friend's face turn to anger. I felt ashamed. It was as if I'd betrayed her, or stolen something from her. Hamza, far from being embarrassed, moved close to me and started whispering endearments, right there in front of her. Mina thought she saw false affection on my part, some sort of cruel game. She shouted, 'Get out of here, man-stealing bitch!' I protested, begged, she screamed at me again, and Hamza took my hand, saying, 'Don't mind her, let's go!' I didn't want to go with him, didn't want Mina to misunderstand, but she refused to hear me. I walked away in tears. When Hamza tried to kiss me again, I slapped his face.

He kept coming back, but I refused to open the door. I wondered how to repair my relationship with Mina, who'd always supported me, who'd rescued me from the distress that sometimes threatened to suffocate me. She was slandering me all over town, calling me a sneaky little bitch, saying that behind my facade of innocence I hid the fangs and fingernails of a witch, that I'd stolen her best friend, her almost-fiancé. The injustice of it cut me to the quick. I spent my days licking my wounds. Then, one evening, I came home to find Hamza sitting on a mat, telling funny stories to my old cousin, who couldn't stop laughing. He did have a sense of humour. It was his *joie de vivre* that finally won me over.

That was the beginning of an idyll that I thought would last. Hamza showered me with affection and gifts. He gave me fine silk scarves, dresses of a quality I'd never dreamed of, shoes, brand-name perfumes... he ushered me into an enchanted world. He furnished my entire house, paved the courtyard, insulated the walls, replaced the doors. My home grew around me until it was unrecognisable. I was a spoiled princess, Hamza the emir of my nights. But the dream soon faded: Hamza's family intervened to stop his spending. There was no question for them of an alliance with a girl of no standing. They threatened to stop his allowance, to cut him off from the comforts he enjoyed, to strip him of their name and to curse him before God and man. His mother sent me a rude letter, to which I didn't reply. I tried to keep hold of him, saying, 'I'll work, you'll work, we'll get married, we won't need anyone, we may not be rich, but we'll be happy, I'll be the best wife there could be!' I thought I could win him back from them, that my heart would mean more to him than money and a crusty old name. But he left: cringing, sheepish, unable to fight for his love, bowed beneath the weight of his family. I despised him, spat in his face when he came to apologise. I understood then that independence and freedom required integrity of both heart and mind. I vowed that I would always have both.

Those few months had given me a glimpse of a different life; one in which no one had to tighten their belt, or stay up late patching worn-out clothes, or worry about putting food on the table or the chill nights of approaching winter. My house was bigger, my nights were longer and quieter, and the senses Hamza had awakened in me refused to go to sleep in the evenings. I began to receive friends and lovers. I turned my own home into a fashionable hangout for all those who, in my too calm and too cautious city, craved spontaneity. I provided a haven for musicians and *griots*, rich gallants and penniless poets, married men hiding from their wives, young executives or businessmen passing through. I found I was a talented hostess, that I knew how to receive every kind of person, and also how to make time for myself. The reality, of course, was that I was a saleswoman. I sold an atmosphere, the promise of encounters and pleasure, and sometimes I also sold myself. I only offered my body for a high price. I clung to my pride, held my head high, believed in my unique charms. I found that, deep inside me, a confidence remained that meant I could refuse people who I found too coarse or prejudiced, too presumptuous that their well-filled pockets or well-fed bellies were enough to get them accepted, or too arrogant, flaunting their beauty while their brains and hearts were empty.

That was the reason I turned down Moustaff, the mayor. He was the most important man in town, part of the old local aristocracy. He was fat, with a thick beard and tousled hair. The dark glasses he always wore concealed a slight squint. He had a sharp voice and dressed in a voluminous *boubou*. He was entirely confident of his power over things and people. He had a near-monopoly over trade in the town, owning half the shops in the Central Market, several residencies and a large herd of cattle. He dominated local politics too, thanks to his money and connections. To him, there was no question I would open my door and my arms to him the minute he gave the signal. When he sent word one evening that he was coming to visit me, and therefore expected me to be alone, I reacted with anger. I screamed at his messenger, 'Tell him that I, Saara, daughter of a poor family, person of no breeding, slut, am not available to see him. Tell him I want nothing to do with him. Tell him I don't give a shit about his fortune or his name!'

Sometimes I found myself drawn to the quality of a voice, an eloquent turn of phrase, a smile. I chased after so many shadows; fleeting visions, passions that existed only in my mind. Time and again, I'd be enchanted by a gesture, the contours of a torso, the twinkle in an eye. Then it would dissipate like smoke. It didn't take long for my lovers to bore me. They'd get jealous, start trying to tie me down. Sometimes they ended it; usually it was me.

Moctar was the last of my illusions, the one I abandoned all the others for. To try to keep hold of him, I borrowed figure-hugging dresses from the kinds of women who were devoted to their men. I spent extravagantly on the finest perfumes, the most alluring outfits, the most sumptuous meals, the most talented musicians. I honed my sense of humour for him, paraded my urbanity. But he ran away too in the end, chased off by the moralising sermons of his family, the raised eyebrows of his friends, the frowns of a milieu that liked to proclaim its virtue while practising injustice and vice every day. Moctar was from a poor background but had always been drawn to appearance and pretence, been fascinated by power and wealth. After he left me, he could often be seen glued to our criminal mayor's side. Moustaff had entrusted him with 'important responsibilities', or at least that was what Moctar said one time when I bumped into him. He looked abashed, ashamed of his desertion, but he didn't linger, reluctant for us be seen together in public. I felt sorry for him, in fact—he was just a poor man who needed a big man's shadow to walk in, a puppet in the hands of a cynic, a wretch who was scared of going hungry, the offspring of the eternally-oppressed who'd been dazzled by the glint of his oppressor. I just hoped he'd forgotten it all: our loving glances, our hands meeting instinctively as we walked, the poems we read together with one voice, all the other memories he didn't deserve, moments too sweet to have been experienced with someone so mediocre. I wished for it all to be erased from his memory, because I'd banished him from mine.

People always singled me out for disapproval, called me immoral, a bitch, a man-eater. It never bothered me, because

I knew their true worth. I knew what lay beneath the flapping *burnous* of their sentences and the floating veils of their false modesty. It didn't stop me from living as I pleased.

Despite everything, I had real friends who I liked and who liked me. They were all eccentrics, but their company suited me. There was Sam the poet, Jid the deaf beggar, Breika the best tam-tam player in the world, Cheibou, Aziza and Zeinab.

Sam strolled through our city, tall and skinny, in a faded *boubou*, with a smile on his lips and honeyed words always ready for anyone who'd hear them. The poems he recited were either memorised or created in the moment. Sometimes they were a bit too long, but they were always good. His favourite themes were love, alcohol and acerbic criticism of all governments; his favourite targets the mayor, whom he called Moustaff the Horrible, and the ruling party, which he called The Monster. Boys crowded around him; girls squeezed hold of him for a little longer than usual when they greeted him. To the elderly and the 'respectable', he was akin to Satan. They cursed him, but his reputation and his well-known family protected him.

Jid was mute but his eyes spoke volumes. He was a beggar, but proud; he accepted alms as his due, refusing large notes and only taking coins, reserving a little dignity for himself. He looked after his mother, who was ill and also mute. I was probably the only person he ever saw socially. He came to see me every day or so, and I gave him tea and a meal. Sometimes we sat talking for hours, using signs, and our eyes, and laughter. Sam said Jid was in love with me, but Sam saw love everywhere.

Breika walked as if on water, and moved through life in

the same way. He was polite, shy, softly-spoken. He pretended to be a good, serious Muslim, but his truth was revealed when he started to play: he became a *jinn*. He could make incredible sounds come out of the taut cowhide of his tam-tam drum. He twirled and jumped around his instrument, gesticulating, shouting, singing. He'd close his eyes, then open them again and wink at his audience. At the end, he'd fall down exhausted, dripping with sweat, kissing the floor and the banknotes that were thrown at him.

Zeinab was a person of both the flesh and the spirit. She had an irrepressible sense of humour and liked to compose short verses of love. This often lured suitors to her, but she never went 'too far'. She'd say, 'I'm saving what's important for my future husband.' We'd laugh about this future husband, who still hadn't shown his face, though Zeinab was approaching thirty.

So, despite the fear that seemed to be stalking every heart and mind in the place, I pushed on with my attempts to stave off tedium and convention. My house remained open day and night. I received many guests, a few lovers in the evenings, people for dinner or for tea. Breika livened up our nights with his tam-tam, his songs and his pantomimes, Cheibou played his guitar, and when he wasn't too drunk, Sam recited his poems. Lekhrouva, who had a beautiful voice, sometimes joined us, and Aziza and Zeinab, always immaculately-groomed, entertained our male visitors with their charms and conversation.

All of this was escapism, of course, and it wasn't enough to distract me from the cloud of anguish that hovered above our city, the fault line running through our pleasure, the worry in all of our eyes. The stories of the haunted mountain kept being told.

Sometimes I'd speak inside my head to my sister, ask her if she remembered when we used to run up the mountain. In the mornings, when our father was still asleep, we'd escape from the neighbourhood and chase after each other, jumping from rock to rock, marvelling at the sight of the sun drenching some slopes and barely caressing others, giving the mountain various faces: blue here, dark there, red up at the top. Huge lizards darted past us, things we didn't know the names of; we heard whistling beneath the stones and the echo of our voices answering us, making us laugh. I often asked her if she remembered all of that, but she never replied.

My little sister Nabila lurked behind all of my thoughts and actions. I called to her during my darkest hours. I knew I should forget her, should confine my pain to some hidden part of me, so it could no longer impact my every living moment. I was the toughest fighter there was, but I couldn't claim to have won that battle. The scars of loneliness and lovelessness still smarted inside of me. I tried to fill the void with my soulless 'clientele'; by enveloping Jid, my beggar friend, in my care, by welcoming Sam, the poet shunned by the 'respectable', by giving hugs to children, by sometimes helping women in need. But my little sister wasn't there and I was alone.

My lovers, my friends, my days spent sleeping and my nights spent partying could never satisfy my longing for arms and a heart to hold me, in an embrace that lasted for longer than an instant. Then one day a letter arrived. It said that my dying mother had asked to see me.

THE SHEIKH

I prayed to God I wouldn't stumble on the rocky roads of life and lose my way. Everything felt difficult. I no longer knew in which direction our caravans were heading. Our oasis had taken on a new aspect some time ago, and my companions and I had failed to notice. Night was upon us before we'd realised the sun had set. I couldn't help wondering whether we were still worthy of our faith; whether we could continue to follow our path, to demand of our followers that they put aside personal concerns and dedicate themselves entirely to others and to the absolute.

I was young, but I'd seen things: men weakening and forgetting themselves, palm groves withering, too-long summers drying up spirits and watering holes. I was no longer sure how to keep marching at the head of my people.

I didn't doubt that I was the person to lead our order: I'd

been chosen to wear the sheikh's turban; I carried the *baraka*, the spiritual benediction of my father, who'd selected Louad as our resting place, and of my grandfather, who'd laid out our path, and of every Sufi sheikh who'd sought and discovered his calling. Still, I was plagued with fears.

Louad was resting after a long day, while I lay awake, tormenting myself. The people of the town slept easily because they'd placed their trust in me. I didn't know how to tell them I had no answers: my head and my hands were empty.

My father had foreseen a future for us. When he arrived in Louad, he knew his *hijrah* had ended. He'd called it the Medina of his heart, a place destined for faith, to be a retreat from the world. I couldn't match his optimism or certainty.

Perhaps we hadn't retreated enough. We'd cast occasional glances at the rest of the world; just to see, to understand. But now the world had been alerted to our presence, and we were of interest to it. Every day, men who knew nothing about our order strolled past our homes, asked us about our lives, pretended to be enchanted by our austere aesthetics. We explained our faith and our truths, tried to help them appreciate our path. They stared quizzically at us, then started to exclaim at the depth of our wells, the size of our fields, the lushness of our palm groves, the fertility of our soil, the flavour of our produce. It's our work, we told them; all we have here is work and prayer; all we ask of our land is that it produces enough for us to eat, so we can continue to follow our path and sing the praises of nature, God and our sheikhs. This land is fed by our love for it, we told them, because it's our promised land, the Medina of our hearts. We repeated this, but they weren't looking at us; they were looking all around, as if Louad were for sale and they might buy it.

My friend José laughed at my fears. He told me the world had no use for us because we had nothing to do with it: we belonged to another century, another era. He added, 'You're already dead, my friend, and nobody even wants your bodies, except me. I like you; I have no idea why.' José was a doctor who came to our oasis every week to treat our sick.

'We like you too,' I told him, 'And we know that, apart from your science, you're completely ignorant. What could an atheist Western doctor possibly understand about a religious brotherhood that he calls a "sect"? You'll see, José, we'll stay alive for a good while longer. Our message will conquer more hearts.'

José laughed again, said, 'You're dreaming, my friend!' He didn't push the discussion any further; he had patients waiting. I was left wondering if what he'd said was true.

Back when I'd first placed my father's turban on my head, people and things still sang for me.

I knew who I was, who we all were, where we belonged. I didn't fear the future, because I believed it was already written on our sacred tablets, that nothing unexpected could ever happen.

I was still a child; I could barely recite the Holy Book, my beard hadn't even grown yet, but I was free from doubt. I'd been told from an early age that I could trust my impulses, that all I had to do was go inside myself and meditate intensely, to better understand them, and to study and recite the scriptures. I learned the Qur'an by heart, as well as our other 'mother books', and I developed by listening, to myself and to others. I internalised the precepts of our faith and our path, and I rarely worried: I had my certainties, and life was waiting for me.

Our oasis was bustling then; a magnet for weary nomads, former city dwellers who'd had enough, ambitious or dishonest public officials, merchants, artisans, *griots*, people who'd fallen on hard times, even some runaway slaves. We also had dreamers, mystics and those who were attracted to our path. They all brought us gifts or sought assurance from us, because all were apprehensive about possible darker days to come. All I had to do was pass my rosary over people's heads and pray loudly; the visitors left contented, the inhabitants of Louad were happy, and everyone obeyed me, or behaved as if they did. We worked our land with only our hands, we tasted only the products of our own labour, and the gifts we received were used to do good everywhere, to bring us closer to others. We helped our faithful who lived far away if they needed it, and we prayed for the whole world.

Of course I was intrigued by the idea of other places. I did have dreams of one day discovering the worlds our visitors came from, of touching the walls of imposing buildings in the tortured cities they described, of seeing those lands where misfortune had settled on them and hope had fled. But I'd not yet earned the right to leave Louad. A sheikh didn't belong to himself: my learning was not over, and until I was of age, I could go nowhere without the consent of the Council of Friends of the Great Sheikh, my father.

Still, my mind teemed with impressions from all the reading I'd done, with partially-remembered snatches of remarkable stories I'd heard without really understanding, and with all kinds of yearnings that I tried my best to ignore.

The hours I spent alone with my mother were my times of greatest joy; the only times I could laugh without restraint. My mother enveloped me with love, sometimes scolded me gently, allowed me to say anything I wanted and completely ignored my status as the sheikh. She listened to me and instructed me to become a reader of hearts: to observe people closely, to try to understand them. She'd say, in the pronounced accent that marked her as being from a distant place, 'Son, every person is a deep sea.' She taught me to be myself, to remain humble, not to be seduced by any kind of power. Another of her sayings was, 'No one lives in the sky, and everyone has their destiny.'

My mother came from a different tribe, a different background and a different world. She'd been born a slave and had been given to my father at a young age to be his companion. When she gave birth to me, the Great Sheikh's first and only male child, her status changed. The women of our tribe had to learn to look at her differently; suddenly she was a sheikh's mistress, almost a queen. But she never abandoned her sceptical way of looking at everything, including our path. The sparkle in her eyes never faded: there was a secret story in them that we all longed to know, and that she would never tell. Even I knew nothing about her childhood. All I had were the sad songs she sang in an unknown language. When I asked her questions, she replied, 'Son, your mother is also a deep sea.'

I had my childhood friends—Lemine, Mohand and the rest—and the hours of rambling and recreation we shared. We composed poems, danced to the forbidden rhythms of the old slave music, winked at passers-by in a way that would be unimaginable later, dreamed of faraway loves and invented salacious stories to excite our youthful lusts. Sometimes, when our fathers weren't around, we'd tell those stories to the young virgins we knew. They'd raise their chins at our impertinence and quiver with pleasure beneath their light veils.

Those were moments of complete freedom for me, before I had to carry the weight of my status. I was just another teenager, one of Louad's occasionally restless boys, dipping the pungent odours of his youth in the murky waters of minor misdemeanours.

There were times of prayer and contemplation too, during which, despite my young age, I was required to take on the role of the sheikh. I was still too young to lead the prayers, but I had to pass on the *baraka*, the benediction bequeathed to me by my forefathers. I'd clasp my hands together, raise my head and appeal to God for faith and joy to reign on the earth, for the sick to be cured, for people to eat their fill, for the rain to fall and for the goodness and knowledge of the Great Sheikh, my father, to enlighten the whole of humanity.

My childhood was regimented, but it wasn't unhappy. I knew the role I had to play and my route had been mapped out for me.

I learned to distinguish between what was my own life and what concerned others, and not to confuse the two: to claim back my freedom when I needed to be free, and to give myself to others when I was needed by them. It seemed simple. But new things were coming to complicate it.

Just a few kilometres from our little settlement, the nearest city was expanding. It was about to encroach on us; to tear at the very fabric of what we held most dear, to suck the lifeblood out of our community, to prey on our people's hearts and minds.

As I grew up, I could see that our world was shrinking; that the universe outside us was closing in; that some of our faithful were leaving and never coming back; that the city people who came with offerings were no longer numerous and left us too soon; that the rains came late when they didn't forget us altogether; and that, for several stifling months, Louad was steeped in inertia. Some people were saying that the sacred power of the Great Sheikh had receded, that it would take time for my own power to emerge, and that in the meantime Louad would suffer.

One day, my father's former companions, the ten members of the Council of Friends of the Great Sheikh, summoned me to see them. 'You're now an adolescent, almost an adult,' they told me, 'soon you'll wear the turban of our path. It's time for our followers in the city, those who can't come here, to see you, to touch you, if possible to speak to you. Also,' they added, 'we have less and less wheat, meat and dates; people are less and less moved by our message; gifts are few and far between. If we are to keep the path of the Great Sheikh alive, we must ensure it is embraced by as many people as possible, and help the poor whenever we can.'

They proposed, if I was willing, that I go to the city for a while, to remind our faithful there of the solidarity that should exist between all those who'd chosen our path. They also wanted me to encourage more guests and to attract more donations, for Louad and for poor people everywhere.

I didn't feel ready to leave home, or perhaps this trip wasn't the one I'd been dreaming of. But I didn't really have a choice: I was still a sheikh-in-training, still belonged in my entirety to my father's ten companions. So I agreed, as I'd been taught to, and went with a few others to live for several weeks in the town.

We took up residence in a large house next to a mosque that was led by an *imam* who shared our path. Every evening, after the final prayer, we'd send our incantations to the heavens, proclaiming the trials of life, our fear of the hereafter and the joys of our faith.

Many city dwellers, disturbed by the new era, came seeking the balm of our certainties. Some of them, drawn back to heaven by love, entered into trances and danced until dawn. The fragrance of God's name began to filter through the stinking atmosphere of the town. We brought the pure air of wide open spaces and simple truths to a world that was beginning to forget them. People brought us their sorrows, their transgressions, their impossible dreams. We were visited by women who'd lost their men, childless couples, men who'd made their money by stealing and lying and now wanted to feel clean, public functionaries seeking promotion, sick people craving remission and people who'd done so much wrong that I lowered my eyes so as not to see too much of them. I welcomed them all in the same way, by calling on them to follow the path of the Great Sheikh, giving them a handful of Louad soil, touching their heads, promising them a place in my prayers and reciting the *Al-Fatiha* to bless the road they were about to take.

The circle of our faithful expanded. I also learned that the town had some astonishing attractions.

On television, I saw a different world. Buildings as big as mountains, grand avenues crawling with vehicles and ostentation. There were so many people who thought the world revolved around them, so much spectacle masquerading as truth, so many needless wars and massacres, so much blood spilled in the name of fatuous beliefs and bloated ambitions. I heard about people who evoked God's name in their hatred of the whole world, used it to preach their own deaths and call for the slaughter of innocents. I couldn't understand this fury, disgust, pride, couldn't see how the men who should have been the wisest, the ones who ruled the world, could accept it. Fortunately, it was not my universe. I was far away from it, and I thanked God I'd been born in Louad and had been shown our path.

I also witnessed some strange customs in the town: people passing in the street but not greeting each other; people insulting each other over minor matters. The air was full of foul smells; beggars in rags were everywhere, pleading for coins. Women with bare arms whom I'd never met before looked me in the eye and smiled.

After prayers, the friends of Louad who lived in the city would take me along on their evening visits. These were interminable tea parties with sad young girls with smiles plastered to their faces, dull conversations and people laughing idiotically for a long time for no reason. Once, they left me alone with a woman. She immediately took off all her clothes. Her scrawny chest made me feel nauseous, so I gave her some money to leave. These strange urban ways were definitely not for me, and I determined to do all I could to protect Louad from them. This was a world, it seemed, that had its own end in sight.

When I turned eighteen, I put on my father's turban and became the sheikh of our path, the chief of our tribe and the humble owner of the whole of Louad and a few kilometres beyond. My kingdom was meagre, but in my eyes it equalled that of David.

I didn't get drunk on my new powers: I knew they relied on the goodwill of other people, and that each of those people, as my mother had told me, was a deep sea; unfathomable and always ready to roar.

I made a point of summoning my father's ten companions often, consulting them on every subject; they were the oracles of our path. I also developed the habit of visiting people in their homes: talking to them, kissing and blessing their children, and listening to whatever they had to say.

I received our faithful visitors in person at the entrance to Louad. I refused gifts from the poorest among them, and even sometimes passed these people a small bundle of dates and other foodstuffs. I wanted to win hearts: my mother had taught me I should seek to be loved, because 'no one lives in the sky and everyone has their destiny'.

Our path grew stronger, the faithful flocked to us, and Louad became a prosperous settlement again. My praises were sung far and wide.

Every Friday, it was my duty to climb to the top of the Mountain of Annihilation and pray there alongside the masters, the select few who'd chosen renunciation. That way I could soak up some of their purity, inhale the musk of the love they bore for the divine. It was no chore for me to do this: I'd spent my whole life savouring and delighting in the powerful poetry that emanated from their passion.

SAARA

I listened to them with patience and respect. They were few, but they had a fire in their eyes that entranced me. Sometimes it also scared me a little. They were the Guardians of the Secret and I was just a humble guard at the gate to the long path to purity, to which they alone held the key. I'd been taught that I owed them devotion and absolute submission.

They lived at the summit of the mountain and only came down for prayers on major festivals, or when they were invited to important gatherings. They didn't take wives, wore only rags and fasted most of the time. They had few possessions—palm groves, fields for crops and ploughing animals—but they gave all that they harvested to the poor, and also made it available to the sheikh and the community in times of need.

The Great Sheikh, my father, had never invited anyone else to visit the masters. He called them 'the first among us', and said the faithful should understand that they were more than followers of the path; they were the path.

I made sure to climb to the top of the mountain at least once a week to pray with them, and to listen when they deigned to give me advice. But I loved life too much to renounce the tastes of women and food the way they did.

When I became a sheikh, I had to choose a wife. The elders asked only that the bride's parents be followers of the path.

My mother had no suggestions. 'Follow your heart,' was all she said. But none of the young girls I knew had a place in my heart. I hadn't met the person the books called my 'flame'. There'd been the odd attraction, lustful feelings that sometimes made my stomach flip, but not the passionate infatuation I'd always dreamed of. I was no Qaïs, the Romeo of my readings, and I hadn't met my Leïla, the Juliet who drove him wild.

After a thousand prevarications, I pronounced the name Mahjouba to my mother's waiting ear. Mahjouba was the daughter of one of my father's ten companions. She was well-educated and very religious, but she also had a smile that sometimes seemed to suddenly break free of the bonds of solemn devotion.

The wedding took place according to the customs of our order: my father's friends gathered and read the sacred *Al-Fatiha* from the Qur'an to seal our union, then all night long the faithful sang hymns to the glory of the prophet and to my father, who'd shown us the path. After that, recent converts went into ecstasies, dancing convulsively, their sweat mixing with blood, until dawn. It wasn't what I would have chosen for my wedding: deep down I would've preferred young people dancing and getting drunk on their joy, local *griots* and happy songs, music, hips swaying and sometimes touching, adolescent laughter, moments of simple pleasure. I dreamed in private of all of that, knowing it was impossible. In Louad, the path reigned, and I was now the sheikh of the path.

Mahjouba was a good wife: pious, generous and respected throughout Louad. She knew how to receive guests, but the spark I thought I'd seen in her had been extinguished by the time we married, snuffed out by convention. All that remained was a capable housewife and a dutiful lover.

The days passed without any major tension or disruption. Louad woke every morning to the rustle of its palm trees and the voice of its *muezzin*, whose call to prayer was a hymn to our serenity.

Of course we often looked to the mountain. We knew that on the other side of it, fear reigned and strange things were happening. This was of little relevance to us, though: the followers of renunciation protected us with their prayers, and the blessing of the Great Sheikh still hung over the skies of our settlement.

Nor did we fear those in power, because we'd given them our pledge. My father had always called for respect for the authorities in power, whoever they might be. He said that the kingdom we desired did not belong here, that the conflicts of this world were of little importance to us, and that any ruler who did not forbid our faith should be given our full support. I made sure we paid our taxes. We participated in financing the election campaigns of the party in power and always voted for its candidates. We received all emissaries of the state, whatever their rank, with respect. We weren't even a whole commune in ourselves, only the least-populated scrap of the commune of Atar, but we mattered to the politicians because our followers were spread throughout the land.

Our only bone of contention with the authorities was the school. We'd discussed it at length with representatives from the Ministry for Education. We'd brought the young children of Louad before these incredulous officials, to show them what they knew. We'd invited the delegation to walk around the oasis and engage our teenagers in conversation. We'd explained that Louad didn't need a school because it already had one. Our children learned the alphabet early on, then the Qur'an, then grammar, then poetry, then theology, then the sacred principles of our path. We paid visiting teachers to come and instruct them in the modern sciences. When the time came, all of our children passed the exams that opened the doors to secondary and higher education. Many of them were now in the towns, working as doctors, engineers, agronomists or teachers. They'd started their education with us, and they came back to see us whenever they could.

We thought we'd been sufficiently convincing, but the administration continued to insist. It was clear that, for them, it was a matter of principle and authority. It was also clear that they'd already made the decision for us.

I invited the ten companions of the Great Sheikh to discuss the issue. The final decision would be mine alone: I was required to go deep inside myself, to listen for the voice of the Great Sheikh that resonated in me. But first I had to gather the opinions of people with knowledge.

The elders were divided. Some thought we should reject this symbol of modernity outright. 'It would be a rejection of our *marabouts*,' said one, 'of our *ulama*, our books, some of them hundreds of years old, written in distant lands, all of the knowledge we've accumulated over centuries!'

'And the messages of the Great Sheikh,' said another, 'the rhythm of our faith! How would we make sure they were passed down to our children? Are we going to allow all of that to fade away while new teachers fill our children's heads with science and foreign concepts? And who's to say the authorities would stop at a school? What might they demand from us next?'

Others were more measured. 'Let them build the school if they want to, let's show them we're ready to co-operate, but let's not send our children to their classes. They'll soon give up on us!'

I spent a long time listening to their arguments. At one point they launched into an erudite debate about religious and secular schools. They explored the theories of various *ulama* on education, and consulted the texts written by the great masters and the Great Sheikh for inspiration.

I'd invited the followers of renunciation to come down from their refuge and join our discussion, but they'd made no response to my invitation. The issue was of little importance to them because it didn't directly involve their faith.

As far as I could see, the questions we were asking ourselves were already out of date: a great storm was approaching from somewhere on the horizon, threatening to blow away our flimsy tents. I'd already seen it at work in all the ugly aspects of the city: the idols, the excess, the riches, the cynicism, the violence. A teacher was nothing, a state was nothing, but behind them was the whole world, and it had turned its gaze on us. We had no means of opposing this unruly *harmattan*. Our path prohibited violence and dictated that we submit to earthly forces, because our Eden lived inside us. How could we halt this march of darkness with nothing but empty hands and loving hearts?

I raised my palms to halt the discussion. I closed my eyes. Everyone froze: this was the moment they'd been waiting for: the sheikh would go inside himself to search for the truth. This would result in a final decision, ending all debate and requiring the faithful to obey.

I thought of nothing, calmed my mind and my senses, hushed all that cried out inside me. I waited for the voice of silence to emerge from the deep abyss, when all had become still and raw. That voice bypassed the intellect: it was the voice of God, transmitted through the *baraka* of my father, of which I would become the receptacle and the echo.

I could hear the expectant inhalations of those around me, could almost sense the swarming of their spirits. I clung tightly to the wave that carried me towards stillness, blackness, then light; the moment when the spirit would fall silent, colours and sounds would fade away, and only the breath would sing in my ears.

I raised my head and opened my eyes to their waiting gazes. 'We'll build the school,' I said. 'No restrictions. We'll build it ourselves. We'll welcome their teachers and their books with open arms.' My tone was both weary and decisive. Then I got up and left the big tent and their murmuring.

I'd known it for some time: our order was not made to reject the world, or to raise our chins in insolence at it. We were sitting singing of peace in a cave that had already been conquered by warlike powers. There would be no new Medina to welcome us. My father had closed the gates of his *hijrah*, his great journey of faith. 'It is in Louad,' he'd said, 'that I have definitively ended my exile and that of those who follow me.' We could neither call for battle nor leave the arena while the hostile forces postured before us. We could only accept their dictates and go back inside ourselves, shelter in our faith in order to survive. At school, the children would listen to their songs; at home we'd teach them ours. Who would win the duel?

I didn't realise then that the school was the prelude to another battle, and that this one would determine our destiny.

One day a car appeared in the valley just as I was going

to the mosque for the midday prayer. A man got out. He wore dark glasses and a frosty expression. He whipped off the glasses as he sauntered towards me. At first I thought he was a foreigner. We had foreign visitors from time to time, and I liked to welcome them, talk to them, learn about their countries and customs, and tell them about our path. But the man called out to me in our own language, in a tone that grated on me.

'Are you the sheikh?'

There was no respect in his voice, only brusqueness and a hint of defiance. He was dressed in a short white shirt and dark trousers. He held his head high in a way I found unnecessarily insolent. He said loudly, 'My name is Moctar. I work for the administration. I've come to talk to you about the new project.' I greeted him humbly and apologised for not being able to talk at that moment: the faithful were waiting for me for the prayer. I called out to one of my people, gesturing towards him. 'He's a guest of God,' I said, then hurried away without looking back, because the call of the *muezzin* had rung out again.

When I returned, he was still standing in the same place. His arms were folded and he was casting contemptuous glances around him. I chastised my house staff: 'Didn't I tell you he was a guest of God?'

'Yes,' they replied, 'but he refused to come in, refused food or drink.'

'I've only come about the projects,' he repeated.

I touched his arm and gently led him towards our tents. 'We are an order, brother,' I said, 'we're traditional, old-fashioned, backward if you like, but we don't impose ourselves on anyone, and here in Louad we have customs. We like those customs to be respected, and everyone who's come here before, from the administration or anywhere else, has always respected them.'

He murmured an apology. We sat down, and for an hour he talked non-stop. I listened as he explained, using expansive gestures, everything I already knew about modern schools, equality, the future and development.

He accepted the tea, dates, milk and couscous served to him. Then he got to his feet.

'I've wasted a lot of time,' he said.

'Here, we don't believe time can be wasted. Every moment is a gift from God. You can live intensely even when you're alone in a vast desert.'

'I come from a different place.'

'I know. Perhaps a different time as well. Our path teaches us to respect all beliefs and all places. The voice of God resounds everywhere.'

'You speak well, Mr Sheikh, but I think differently.'

'I accept your difference. But not "Mr Sheikh".'

'What should I call you?'

'Just "Sheikh". Or "subject of God", or "younger brother", because I think you're older than me. Or by my first name if you like, which is Qotb.'

'I'll call you whatever you want, but first I'll tell you our plans.'

'I'm listening, brother.'

'First, there's the school.'

'We've agreed to that. The next time you come back, you'll find the classrooms ready.'

'The administration will build them!'

'In Louad, we do everything ourselves, whenever we can.'

'Fine. I'll tell my superiors. The other thing is that the

government has decided to build a dam here. The foreign company that will build it has just been chosen.'

'I thought you only came about the school.'

'About the school, that you were so slow to accept, and also about this project, which has been given the go-ahead by the administration and will soon be started.'

'This place belongs to God and to our path.'

'It belongs first and foremost to the state. You yourself, although you're a sheikh, are only a custodian of it, and a very provisional one at that. I'm here to warn you that we won't accept your systematic opposition to what will make the population happy.'

'I don't think we have the same notion of happiness.'

'But it's our notion of happiness that's more important, and it involves education and making the most of our opportunities, especially agricultural ones.'

'Here we believe first and foremost in Heaven, and we look for God in everything, especially ourselves.'

'God has nothing to do with this.'

'God for us is a presence!'

'You'll excuse me, but I must go now. I didn't come to argue, only to inform you.'

'Be sure to tell the authorities who sent you that we accept the school, that we'll build it ourselves, and that we thank them and will pray for them. But tell them that as far as the dam is concerned, I remain unconvinced. This is a place of faith. We've retreated here to pray and to follow our path. There aren't many of us, and we have enough water to meet our needs and to grow our crops; we work only with our own hands. Our oasis is therefore not suitable for these "development projects", as I believe you call them. They'd certainly be more useful and better accepted elsewhere.'

'The dam has already been approved by the authorities. It's not just for you—it will benefit the whole region.'

'But this land belongs to us. It was my father and my grandfather, with their followers, who carved out this road between the mountains, who planted these palm trees, who dug these wells, and who dedicated the whole area to the work of their hands and to their prayers.'

'Actually, the land doesn't belong to you. No administration has ever granted you any title to it.'

'We were living on it before your administration came into existence!'

'That's irrelevant. Even if you did legally own the land, the administration has the right to take it away from you. It's called "*force majeure*". Do you know about that?'

'I only know about justice and the fact that you're threatening the serenity of a community that's always respected order.'

'It's in the hands of the administration now. You can't oppose it, sheikh or not. In a few days the mayor himself will come and explain it to you. I have to go now, Mr Sheikh.'

'May peace go with you.'

I came home after that conversation completely drained. That insolent, uneducated man could only be the harbinger of trouble. He had no respect for our path, yet he wanted a school for our children; he'd never been here before, yet he was proposing to unknown foreigners that they should carry out projects in the Louad Valley. The unnecessary dam, it was suddenly clear to me, would be our death-knell; it would spell exile for our faith, something that was forbidden to us, because the Great Sheikh had said, 'Louad is destined for the faith, only the faith.' It would be impossible for us to accept the dam. Why had I not been warned of this madness in advance? Why was I now being informed of the imminent start of the project as if we had no say in the matter? Should I climb the mountain, listen to the followers of renunciation, summon the masters, or should I wait? How could I have accepted this treatment? Why didn't I dismiss that man on the spot?

I couldn't stay still, I paced round and round in circles as I searched for an answer. I decided to take a walk.

I bumped into José, who'd just been to see my mother. 'José!' I cried, 'They want to build a dam here, in our oasis!'

José looked around him, as if to check everything was still real. 'A dam? What for? Well, it's true your oasis would be ideal for something like that; it's a beautiful valley after all, and in fertile years it must be very profitable.'

'But this valley belongs to us, to our path!'

'That's true, my friend, this land belongs to you, but what you don't understand, sheikh that you are, and what I, the retarded Westerner, as you call me, understand perfectly, is that these people have already stolen your whole country. They won't think twice about grabbing a promising piece of land like Louad.'

'I can't accept it!'

'You'll have to.'

'What?'

'You'll have to accept it because they have strength and the law—their law—on their side.'

'I have God on my side.'

'You know what I think about that.'

'Yes, but you also know the strength of faith.'

'Ah, faith…'

'The truth, if you prefer.'

'They have the truth of weapons. That's all they need.'

'I won't let them!'

'How are you going to stop them?'

'I don't know yet.'

'Your path forbids violence. I don't see what you can do.'

'Perhaps we'll have to wait until the mayor arrives to find out more. Perhaps he and I will understand each other. Goodbye, my friend, I'm going to pray.'

'And I'm going to visit a few more sick people before I go. Your mother is better.'

'I prayed for her!'

'And I treated her!'

THE BEGGAR

All I had to do was squeeze my eyelids shut, ignore all the sounds, the scents, the shocks of the world around me, press them down slowly until they were submerged, then wait.

I'd see my mother. All eyes turned towards her. Her thinning hair expertly braided; her smile shining from the depths of her dark features; her words bubbling up from the deep well of her suffering. Beautiful, just like Saara. I'd see myself as a child; people patting my head and pinching my cheeks, smiling and offering endearments, sending me off to school with a satchel on my back. I'd see myself in the evenings, being pampered and put to bed early. I'd see trees everywhere, covering the barren land with a dense canopy of shade. I'd even see grass, cushioning my feet as I raced frantically towards the sea, which was just behind a dune: soon I'd be feeling the waves caressing my feet, smelling the sea spray, touching the ocean's skin.

I couldn't close my eyes all the time, and my dream-pictures didn't always last. Sometimes they were ripped away by the claws of the villainous forces that lurked all around me: in the dark, squalid hut, in danger of collapsing, where I lay, in the foul stench that pursued me, in the sound of my mother's unending pain. I didn't want her to fall silent; I feared it. If she was silent, everything else would be silent too, the whole world would burn and die. I wept at the thought of never seeing her again. She fidgeted and shifted in her corner. Nothing helped, not the *marabout's* talisman, not Saara's pills, not the acacia leaves, not my prayers. My mother's fever wouldn't break. She shivered with her entire body. I'd get up and go over to her, to answer her babbling, unintelligible to anyone but me. I'd embrace her, make her drink the goat's milk she didn't like, eat the stale bread she chewed for too long, have a glass of tea to soothe her unquenchable thirst. It pained me to see her suffer. She'd been given nothing in life except suffering. Unless you could count me.

One morning, I suspected my mother would keep sleeping for a long time. All night she'd done nothing but moan and touch my face. She was trying to imprint my features on her hands; she was afraid to leave me, and she dreamed of taking me with her to the place where she'd be going, soon perhaps, so we could be together always. But what if there was no place, no love, no togetherness? What would I do alone, in the dark mazes of oblivion?

I prepared to go into town, to smile at people and beg. That was our job, every day, to beg, smile, nod and agree. With time, I'd learned. I didn't look people in the eye any more, because I didn't know how to beg with my eyes. I just stammered shyly, head lowered, extended hand trembling. People gave me small coins, sometimes a loaf of bread, sometimes a handful of dates and sugar and sometimes nothing but a swear word. I accepted everything.

They called me Jid, the son of crazy Nana. Some people said I wasn't hers, that she'd stolen me when I was a baby, but that was nonsense. There was no doubt I was her son: you only had to look at the way she protected me when I was small, baring her teeth when anyone came near; the way she whimpered at night when I was ill, alone in that remote hovel; the way she ran her hands gently over my face, caressing every rough spot, every pimple, discovering me anew every day.

I was Nana's son, but it was true that I had no father. Who could have told me about him if I did? My mother was deaf and mute. Nobody knew anything about her. She'd appeared a long time ago in Atar, with a baby in her arms. No one had any idea where she'd come from and no one had even seen her face: she knew how to scream, and her sharp nails would dig into the face of anyone who tried to tear off her veil. She spent her days begging and her evenings in the home she'd built for us, a hut hidden amidst thorny trees. Nobody knew how she'd built the hut. Nobody knew how she sensed the presence of others near her. My mother was full of mysteries. Even I knew nothing about her. There were evenings, when I was small, when I'd cry, shout, torment her, demand that she tell me, with gestures, lines in the sand, in any way she could, something of our story. At first her face would remain expressionless, like marble, then she'd begin to moan, then tears would streak down her cheeks. I'd hug her and swear every time never to ask again. A few days or weeks later, the whole thing would repeat itself. Did my mother even know who she was? I wasn't sure she did, or maybe the secret was buried so deeply inside her it had been lost. How could she have told me about her past if she'd forgotten it herself? I became a master of the sign language we shared, that belonged to us alone, but we only ever used it to refer to everyday activities: coming, going, sleeping, eating, loving, hating; the actions we conjugated in our grammar were those of our day-to-day. The only words I ever heard my mother pronounce almost distinctly were her name, 'Nana', and mine, 'Jid', which she released with a sudden movement of her whole body, as if she'd swallowed the bones of the sounds and was expelling them with force. Was she really called 'Nana'? Maybe that was the only sound she could make, so she had to own it.

I once overheard Med, the driver, telling his friends that during his travels around the region, he'd asked about my mother and received no answer; nobody knew her. People had just kept it to themselves, I assumed, refused to admit she'd ever been in their miserable little corner of the desert. They'd disowned her because she was a burden, no use to anyone, perhaps because she'd given birth to me. Was I the product of rape? Certainly. Forbidden love? Certainly not. Child abduction? Impossible. Even Baba, the restaurant owner, had once said, 'Remember when she was breastfeeding him? That's the only part of her body we've ever seen, the breast she took out when she sat in the shade of that wall to feed her child.' I'd also heard him say that she must have come from a long way away and that I must have been around two months old when we arrived. I would have liked to ask Baba for more information, but I couldn't—I was deaf and dumb, after all.

My mother really was deaf and dumb, but sometimes, on fine nights, when I wasn't too exhausted and was enjoying life a little, I used to feel sure she could hear me. I'd spread a mat on the stony ground, sit down to make tea and sing her the soft music that I pretended not to hear all day. Her eyes would brighten with all the smiles in the sky. She'd take off her veil and her face would flood with light. My mother's face was beautiful, and I was the only person who ever saw it. The chickenpox scars that dug tiny craters in her cheek didn't spoil it. She had a long, finely-curved nose, lips that were full but not too thick, teeth that were white, in spite of what she'd endured, a broad forehead and large eyes. At first you'd think you could see the sunset reflected in those eyes, but it would disappear as soon as you approached. She had a small scar on her cheek, a gash from an accident, perhaps. But she was beautiful.

Why was she so determined to hide her face? Perhaps she didn't like it because it didn't feel like part of her anymore.

They felt far away, the days when she'd drag me by the hand to go begging. We'd crisscross the whole city. She'd shake the big tin pot she carried on her arm, the handle rattling like a complaint. People would come out of their houses and fill the pot with rice, peanuts, couscous and pasta, all mixed up. Sometimes they'd hand me a coin, which I'd grip tightly. My mother walked with small, cautious steps, so as not to stumble. I tried to make her speed up, but she was used to this stuttering pace, as hesitant as her life. She could feel my presence and always knew if I'd moved away from her side, if someone had addressed me or beckoned me over to take a coin. She never let me go far. I longed to escape from her. I'd watch other children playing and ache to join them. On the rare occasions when I did though, all I got were insults and blows. 'Bastard, son of a madwoman!' they'd scream, 'You stink!' I'd run away, to catch up with my mother. I learned to hate those sons of bitches, and I never stopped hating them. Alem was the only one who was ever happy to play with me, and that was only because he hated losing at marbles and I always let him win. I rarely had marbles to play with anyway: the coins I was given weren't enough for those.

My mother was also in a sense my jailer: deprived of her own senses, she prevented me from seeing the world, from living in the way other people did, from being a child. She did it to protect me, but I didn't know that at the time and was always trying to get away. The reproach in other people's eyes would send me back to her. Even when I wasn't standing in her shadow, I was still always 'the son of the mute beggar'. When I went back, I'd find in her arms, and in the moistness of her eyes, a warmth that could comfort me in spite of everything.

Then came the time when my mother couldn't walk anymore. All she could do was drag herself to water to drink, or to the toilet. She was like an ancient reptile, worn down by years and misery.

There was a particular day when we both suffered a great deal. My mother fell into a huge ditch that had been carved out of our path by stonecutters. I was behind her, and I saw her disappear as if she'd been swallowed up, snatched away by this unexpected void. I started shouting at the top of my voice and running around like a madman. I hurtled down the dark, stony path, railing against the city below and the heavens above for ignoring my mother's suffering. My cries for help were echoed back to me by the mountain. Eventually, two brawny black men appeared. They leaned over the ditch, then one of them went down, lifted my mother and passed her to the other one, who gently pulled her up. She was unconscious and covered in blood. I wailed and cried, terrified that she was dead, that I'd lost everything that tied me to life. One of the men put her on his back. I followed them. They didn't know the town, so I showed them the way to the clinic. When we got there, they laid her down on a very white bed and went back outside. I bathed my mother's face with some mineral water they'd left us, and she regained consciousness. I replaced her veil so her face was covered; I knew she'd want that. Finally, a nurse arrived. 'The mute woman, the poor thing!' he exclaimed. He examined her wounds, then wrote a prescription and handed it to me. I shook my head, so he rubbed something on the wound. My mother moaned, and I realised she must be in a lot of pain, because usually she could withstand anything. 'Please be gentle with her,' I said to the nurse. He bandaged both of her knees and handed me another prescription. I accepted this one, to please him. The two black men were still waiting outside. They took it in turns to carry my mother back to our hut. The next day they came back with the nurse's prescription and some more medicine, gave me a few coins and left. I never saw them again. I wondered if they were good *jinn* sent to earth to save my poor mother.

Sam explained to me later that they were probably migrants from a distant place, passing through on their way to the Mediterranean, working a little when they could, just enough to sustain themselves until the next stopover. Those people never stayed anywhere for long, in case the police arrested them and sent them back home. I often thought about those two men after that. When I saw a boat carrying migrants on Saara's television, I thought I recognised them. I prayed for their safety and that of all the others with them.

I didn't actually know how to pray. I pretended to do it, but I'd never been taught what to say; I'd only picked up bits and pieces. On Fridays, I'd mumble a few words behind the others while I was waiting for the prayer to finish so I could hold out my pot. But I knew I wouldn't go to hell: Saara had told me that people who'd suffered a lot in this world were well-received in the hereafter. She also told me that God and love lived in each person's heart. I wasn't certain that Saara and religion saw eye to eye, but I loved Saara very much, and she was always right.

The day after her accident, my mother did nothing but whimper. I gave her the medicine, took off her bandage, washed the wounds with hot water, then washed the bandage and put it back on, as prescribed. I stayed beside her for two days. We still had some rice, milk, pieces of stale bread and biscuits, and I went down to get water. On the third day, there was nothing left to eat, so I took my mother's pot and went to beg.

From that day on, I no longer spoke, and I pretended I couldn't hear. That was how I became 'the little deaf-mute beggar'. People were confused at first, saying, 'But you used to speak!' Then they decided it must be a hereditary disease that had suddenly emerged. After a while they didn't think anything at all.

I knew the trade; I'd drunk it with my mother's milk. I knew every gesture, every look, every prayer: 'May God repay your kindnesses; may God grant you long and beautiful days; may God bless your children; may God pardon your ancestors…' I said all of that without saying it, by reaching my hands to heaven, shaking my head, looking beseechingly at people, devising gestures to say everything I'd heard the other beggars saying with words.

The only thing I wasn't really able to suppress was my laughter. When I felt like laughing, I'd clamp my mouth shut and run as far away from people as I could. Then I'd laugh until my guts knotted and my voice croaked and my cheeks became loose and my eyes streamed with tears. Sometimes I just wanted to talk, to express myself, to shout out my feelings. It was as if there was a volcano inside me: noises rumbled in my belly and tried to erupt out of my mouth. When I felt that happening, I ran until I was breathless, to the outskirts of the city, and there I started to shout and dance and scream. I filled the air with words, repeated all the thoughts I'd had during the day: that Moustaff the mayor and his son deserved to die a thousand times over; that I'd kill them one day; that Salem the shopkeeper was greedy and dishonest; that Rama was a bitch; that in this whole heartless town, Saara and Sam the poet were the only people I loved.

The road to the city always felt long. I rushed to cross the fields, ravaged by drought and neglect, and the crumbling desert pavement of rocks and stones that we called the *reg*. Sharp pebbles dug into my bare feet. Stunted trees loomed up before me like ghosts, and tiny creatures who lived in the depths of their dead trunks swarmed around me. I closed my eyes as I sprinted across the *battha*, the river of sand that separated the city from the fields. Beyond that was the Central Market, where everything happened; where the people were, with their shouting, their money and merchandise, their eyes filled with greed. There, ignored by everyone, I melted into the crowd and made my way to the heart of the maelstrom. I found my place beside Zeghlana's stall and reached my hand out to the people walking by. Zeghlana always had her child in her arms and often fed him. Her teats were as big as melons after the winter. From a big pot, she drew the quantity of couscous requested by each customer. She had a kind word for all of them, asking about their families, telling jokes. The customers sometimes slipped me a coin when she gave them their change. Zeghlana didn't stay long at the market, though. She also had another job, cleaning rich people's houses.

I stopped in front of Med's shop too. He sent me away, but I kept coming back because there was shade there. Cars stopped and the passengers didn't even get out; Med or his employees went to take their orders. Then I could ask the drivers for charity, which they didn't always give.

I couldn't go everywhere. I was forbidden by the other beggars from begging at crossroads: they shouted at me as soon as I got close, 'Come near here and you're dead!' They made a sign, a finger slicing the throat.

I was usually with another young beggar whose name was Mama. I didn't want to be, but she clung to me like something sticky. I pushed her away, insulted her, even threw little pebbles at her. Nothing put her off. She followed me everywhere. It was irritating. Mama was not at all beautiful: her eyes were too big, her forehead too wide, her mouth toothless, often with saliva around it. She always had her baby on her back. But there was something about her voice that made people turn their heads. When she cried out, 'Charity! God will repay you!' passers-by came and gave her coins. She smiled back at them then and looked at me as if to say, 'See!' She always offered to share her takings with me, but I refused. When I walked away, she still followed me. Sometimes I had to run to lose her.

Mama had a troubled history. She was abandoned as a child on the outskirts of town and was taken in by a poor old woman, a former slave who sold her withered charms for a few pennies to the local tramps. The two of them lived in a disused hangar near a military garrison. When the old lady died, Mama was left alone; nobody wanted her because she was dirty and ugly, and because her big eyes were said to be those of a witch. When my mother was still going out begging, Mama had already been on the streets for a long time. She crossed the town with surprising speed, and her voice already displayed that quality that made kind people take notice. When she got pregnant, people asked her how it had happened, because she'd never been seen with a man. She told them young men from the town often attacked her at night when she was alone in the hangar and raped her. Saara distrusted this version of events: 'She likes men, you can tell!' she laughed.

I was quickly annoyed by Mama's beatific smile, her odour of rancid couscous, and the excessive, overbearing sympathy she showed me. Saara drove me crazy when she said, 'Mama's in love with you.' I pretended not to hear, but it made me angry. 'She's insane', I'd say, by pointing my finger at my temple. I constantly plotted ways to get her away from me. I never dared hit her, though the idea occurred to me.

Once, when I insulted her too fiercely and made her cry, I even felt obliged to hold her in my arms, to stroke her head a little and press her fleshy body against mine. It seemed to give her ideas: she gripped me tightly when she felt the uncontrollable desire rising up in me. I pushed her away and never allowed her to touch me again.

Whenever I saw someone handing Mama a large note, I'd rush over and shake my head to warn her not to take it. She'd give the note back and look at me, always the same way, a little bewildered. Eventually she learned only to accept small change. 'We're beggars after all,' I'd tell her.

In the evenings, if I was in a good mood, I'd sometimes let her come back to the hut with me. She'd wash my mother and plait her hair, sometimes she'd cook for us. Then I'd send her away, before she started wanting more. One day, when she wouldn't stop chattering, a lot of nonsense about weddings and parties, about me holding her in my arms, and I don't know what else, I shouted, 'Will you shut up for a minute?' She stopped, stunned, and stared at me. 'Yes,' I said, 'I can speak and I can hear, but if you tell anyone, I'll tear off your skin and throw it in the stinkiest dustbin; I'll gouge out your eyes; I'll cut off your breasts and feed them to Saara's cat; I'll rip out your tongue! I spoke against my will because the sound of your chattering drove me to it, but I won't talk to you or anyone else again, only to my mother when we're alone. Do you understand?' When she'd recovered from her shock, she lowered her head and I saw tears in her eyes. Then she pulled herself together and carried on cooking as if nothing had happened. I knew then that she wouldn't say a word.

Yes, there were times when I was on the verge of forgetting myself, of throwing out a word, smiling in a way that betrayed understanding, turning when I was called. I had to keep reminding myself I was deaf and dumb, for everyone: Mama, Saara, even myself. It had to stay that way. I often felt words, noises, and furious growls inside me; sometimes felt a strong desire to shout, 'Shit!' at a man, a woman, or humanity in general. The sounds got as far as my throat, then stuck there. They jostled against each other but they never crossed my palate; I'd set up a permanent red light there. They sank back down and swarmed around in my belly instead.

I did talk to my mother when we were alone in our hut. I told her the people in the city believed our mountain was haunted by *jinns*. It wasn't true, there was nothing but my fear there at night. I laughed at their idiocy, but it also meant no one disturbed us. I told my mother what was on my mind: how beautiful and generous Saara was and how much she liked me; how Sam the poet was a friend of Saara's and liked me too; how Kory the fat beggar attacked and hated me for reasons I didn't understand; how I stole Mehdi's marbles whenever I found him alone, and he shouted but did nothing, his big brother once said some nasty things about Saara, so... and about how Cheibou always smiled and walked like a woman but was also Saara's friend. I told my mother that I knew Rama, the gem-seller who always talked badly of Saara, was the lover of Selman the butcher; that he gave her meat every day and visited her in the evenings to smell all the beautiful perfumes she had. I knew that Mehmed the *sharif* sold alcohol in big Coke bottles—Sam said that in front of me—and that Saidou, the little bookseller, was a communist and an atheist. I didn't know what that meant, but when Hamod the *muezzin* said it, he preceded it with the word 'dangerous'. I knew all of that and more, because I was deaf, so they all said whatever they liked in front of me.

My mother, on the other hand, really was deaf, but she did know when I was talking to her. Her eyes could embrace me more tightly than any arms. I saw flashes, like lightning, in them, and words on her speechless lips, and music in her tentative gestures.

My mother knew Saara. She used to take me to the front of her house when I was small, and Saara would come out when she heard the sound of my mother's pot or my cries. She always had a few coins and a meal ready for both of us. She invited us in, but my mother always declined. We ate in the street and wiped our plates clean before returning them. Saara told me I should always be obedient and kind to my mother. I promised her I'd do anything she asked; that was when I was still talking.

When the sun rose high above our heads and people were holed up in their homes so they didn't burn to a crisp, so their brains didn't burst and drive them mad; when even the tarmac on the roads was melting, and all the beggars had fled the overheated pavements, I often went to Saara's house. Saara was my resting place, my watering hole, my refuge from the city's clutches. I was never in the way there: she had a big house and a huge courtyard with a beautiful palm tree at the centre where I could sit in the shade. She'd come out and talk to me, hold my hand, call me her 'little friend'. It was as if she suspected I wasn't deaf or dumb. I showed her my friendship through dancing gestures, which made her laugh. I loved seeing the joy in her eyes and watching her majestic body move. Saara was beautiful. She had eyes that beckoned you to die and cheeks as smooth as a baby's and a voice that would make anyone dance. She invited me into her living room, but I always refused. I was just a beggar.

Lots of people visited Saara's house: women who wore lots of make-up and chattered constantly, well-groomed men with fancy cars. Sam, the poet, was often there. I liked him a lot: he talked to me as if I could hear him, recited his poems, then looked at me as if he knew I'd understood. He often brought me a cake, dripping with cream, that he'd kept for too long, which spoiled its taste a little. Sam said whatever he felt like; he was a little bit crazy. Saara said, 'He's an original,' which perhaps meant the same thing. I liked him anyway.

In the evenings, there were parties in the courtyard. Saara and her friends would lay out large rugs. I sometimes helped them. Then the crowds arrived: Breika with his tam-tam, Cheibou with his guitar, Lekhrouva with her beautiful singing voice. Everyone shimmied and laughed, and the ladies got kissed on the mouth, and Sam sang his poems and Cheibou wiggled his hips like a girl. I never stayed for long: I was scared that the music would betray me and I'd start singing. I was scared of worrying my mother, too. Then, after what happened, I was also scared of the night.

The terror of that night never left me. Remembering it sent me into a whirlwind, then it was hard for me to pull myself together, not to tremble, not to cry. I didn't say anything about it to my mother, or Saara, or anyone else. How could I explain that I'd become lost, that I'd almost gone under, almost ceased to exist? They were drunk, they smelled bad, they were laughing very loudly. They handed me a note, and as I reached to take it, they pulled me up. I struggled, they hit me, and then they tortured me, burrowed shame into me, and I screamed and no one came. I didn't recognise all of them, those monsters, but I recognised him. I kept silent about it because he was a respected man, a rich man's son, and I was a filthy, worthless little beggar. Who would believe me? They'd say I was doing it for the money, and maybe they'd send me and my mother away. But the little beggar never forgot. I saw him walking around, his head held high, showing his gleaming teeth to the people he passed. When he saw me, he looked through me, as if there was nothing there.

SAARA

I'd never imagined for a moment that my mother might exile herself in Louad, that village-oasis that was at once so close and yet so far, and so strange, ruled by an ancient sect. Known for the sweetness of its dates, the flavour of its vegetables and the singularity of its inhabitants, Louad was a few kilometres away from us and light years from the rest of the universe. People from Louad were instantly recognisable: they walked on tiptoe, spoke in whispers, dressed in the cheapest fabrics—if they weren't literally wearing rags—and were always mumbling indistinct prayers. The only people who ever went to Louad were the followers of their guru. It lay just behind the mountain, but to get there you had to go round the mountain: sixty kilometres of rocky roads, several hours of being bumped around.

My mother had chosen to move there, to embrace the faith

of a sect that frightened me, to live in total devotion, turning her back on the world, including her own daughters. It hurt me to discover that. I didn't see how someone could abandon their children to a violent father and claim to be a believer. I was so resentful that at first I was determined to ignore the news—I told myself I'd never had a mother. But I couldn't block out the niggling feeling that I might be missing out on something essential. Perhaps my mother had just suffered too much, grown too old. Perhaps she needed me. I tried to brush such thoughts aside and forget again, telling myself that the people of Louad had chosen death: they refused life by banishing the slightest pleasure, they knew only God, the sheikh and their prayers. What use could a woman of the world like me be in a place like that? If only my little sister were with me!

There was no point pretending, though: a longing for my mother ran through me: a desire to touch her face and hands, to smell her arms, to hear her voice, which I'd forgotten, to comb her hair, which had surely turned white. There were also the sorrows I wanted tell her about, the bitterness, the suffering my sister and I had endured because of her desertion. If I went to her, I could let out the angry words I'd only ever whispered to myself. But would I really have the chance to confront her? Wasn't she about to die? Perhaps I'd save her, bring her back home with me. Perhaps we'd learn to love each other, and my sister would join us, and we'd be a family again. I'd forgive, forget, and perhaps I'd be able to look into her eyes with happiness again.

I entrusted my old cousin to Zeinab, closed up my house and hired a good 4x4 with a driver. It would take a few hours, I thought, a trip of a day or two in total, at most.

The drive was arduous, the mountain interminable, the car tossed about by the huge stones, bumped into deep potholes. It lurched as it searched for a way through, but the driver was skilful and had taken the route before. The hardest part was finding the passage that led through this rocky world to Louad. Eventually we found it, and then, from the top of those high ramparts, I found myself looking down on my mother's place of exile. Louad was nestled in a valley surrounded by mountains. At first all I could see was the huge peak that rose up behind it towards the blue sky, strangled by dunes, with two huts clinging to its slopes. Palm trees swayed in the gentle breeze, neat enclosures protected crops, and then the houses appeared, lined up in rows, and to the far north, a large building backed against a mosque surrounded by tents. 'Louad, the Eldorado of the hermits,' said the driver, sniggering. But a plunge down into the rocks still awaited us; we had to descend through a narrow, helter-skelter pass, the car shaking and jolting, the tyres squealing, the driver swearing. 'They built this road with their own hands,' he said, half-admiring, half-infuriated.

It was afternoon and the village was asleep. There was nobody to be seen on the only street. The houses all looked the same, made of stone and clay, with the same blue-painted doors, white walls and low windows almost touching the ground. There were lots of immaculate, well-kept tents. The silence was broken only by a loudspeaker broadcasting suras. We stopped in front of the big building, a long terrace with an expanse of wall and numerous windows. There was no one around. It must have been the sheikh's house. A man emerged hurriedly from a tent and came towards us, opening his arms. He spoke words of kindness, a well-rehearsed refrain, some sort of protocol of the sect. He invited us in. 'No,' I replied, 'we're looking for the house where Lalla lives, an elderly sick woman. She's my mother.' The man froze, stared at me for a moment as if he'd only just noticed me, then pointed towards a house at the other end of the town, 'Our mother Lalla is no longer ill,' he said, 'she suffers from nothing. She's in bliss.' He walked away. I tried to make sense of his words: was she cured, or was she dead?

A group of children were standing outside the house. They stared at us as if we were Martians. Two women covered their faces as soon as we approached. I got out of the car and rushed inside. I couldn't stand it any longer; impatience and confusion raged inside me. The internal courtyard was full of people. Young girls were handing out drinks, women were chanting prayers and waggling their heads. I understood immediately. Surprisingly, considering I'd never really known my mother, I felt an enormous emptiness, a sensation like lava rising up to my head, then pouring out in sobs. It was my childhood that was escaping from me: the years of suffering, the long lost hours, the blind groping for love, the tenderness that disappeared too soon, the fumbling around the walls looking for the door to oblivion, the never-fulfilled expectation of a mother's warmth. I, who had always been so strong, unravelled abruptly.

A woman took me in her arms and offered soothing words. I heard someone say, 'This must be her daughter.' The woman holding me kept repeating phrases: 'She left without suffering; she loved you; you mustn't cry; we don't mourn death here.' I heard another woman say, 'She's from the world of ignorance! She's crying over death, and she's richly dressed. It's not decent!' The first woman murmured a few words. The courtyard immediately emptied.

We were alone. When I raised my head to look at the woman, I realised with a shock that she was blind.

'I'm Salma, your mother's cousin and friend,' she said in a soft voice. 'We've lived in this house for a long time, we stayed together over the years, and I loved her very much. I was with her until the last moment. We've just buried her. The sheikh himself and the whole of Louad prayed over her body. She was a saint.'

'I don't care about her saintliness! I wanted to see her, just see her. I can't even remember her face!'

'She often spoke to me of her daughters.'

'But she left us!'

'No, no. It was just that she'd promised.'

'What do you mean, promised?

'Your father made it a condition of the divorce that she would never try to see you again.'

'No one told me that! Why did she agree to that?'

'Despair. A desire to be rid of a miserable union. She always regretted it. When your father died, she hoped you'd come to her, because she couldn't come to you.'

'But we were so young, so alone…'

'She prayed for you.'

'That wasn't enough!'

'It can be enough, at least in our eyes.'

'It's too late now.'

'Nothing is ever late for those who believe.'

'I'm from a different world.'

'I know that. It doesn't change anything.'

'I'm going to go. There's a car waiting for me.'

'It can wait for a few days, or it can leave without you. You must pray at your mother's grave. You must accept condolences from those who loved her. You must receive the sheikh's blessing.'

'I don't know anyone here and I don't need to be blessed.'

'You'll do it for your mother, or for me—her cousin. Her sister really.'

'I won't stay long.'

'Three days, at least.'

'Why three days?'

'It's our tradition. You stay with your loved ones for at least three days after a bereavement.'

'It's not bereavement I feel. It's abandonment.'

'I understand, my daughter, but you will stay. I ask you. I beg you, even.'

I looked up again and saw those eyes in which the fires had gone out, white hair spilling out of a thick veil, a face wrinkles hadn't made ugly and that was showing real distress, and a smile that tried to belie the silent pain. Salma took my hand and led me into a clean room, furnished with a large mat, lots of pillows and a few light mattresses. She sat me down gently. As if by magic, several women entered the room. They kissed my head and prayed aloud for my mother's soul. The courtyard filled with people again. Their religious songs rose to the heavens. I no longer knew where I was.

The chanting continued until late at night, only stopping when it was time for the evening prayer. I lay prostrate, unable to grasp the spirit of this liturgy, unable to accept the idea of my presence in the midst of it, or of my mourning. Salma brought me a plate of couscous, which I couldn't touch, then

68

invited me to sleep in the courtyard, in the open air. She moved around the house with surprising ease, not needing to touch the walls or reach out her hands. A mat with two blankets and two pillows on top of it had been laid out for me. To escape the heat, we would sleep under the stars. I gazed up at the sky, thought I could read furious designs there.

Salma told me my mother had come to join her just after the divorce, and that during the early years she'd hidden herself away for fear of her former husband. The two cousins had known each other since childhood, but Salma's family had embraced the path laid out by the late sheikh and had 'emigrated', as she put it, to Louad. Salma had been one of the late sheikh's wives, but had borne him no children. 'The sheikh had a daughter with another wife, Seyda, who you'll certainly meet tomorrow, and a son with a concubine given to him by a Malian sheikh. That son is our present sheikh, the one who's been crowned with the *baraka* of his forefathers. You'll meet him too. He's a person of humility, knowledge and virtue.' She explained to me that Louad was a gift from God, a sacred resting place for the followers of the path, that it was protected by the character of the sheikh, the wisdom of his father's ten companions, and the purity of the followers of renunciation. The latter had abandoned all earthly pleasures and lived high up on the mountainside.

'In Louad, we turn our backs on a lot of the superfluous things you have in the city. I should warn you, my daughter, that here there are no telephones, televisions or cinemas. Nothing is allowed to distract us from what gives meaning to our lives: prayer and work.' I thought of my friends, Aziza and Zeinab, who often had their ears glued to their phones, who were crazy about music and TV shows and who'd given up none of the joys of this world. I recalled our lively evenings, our friend the poet, and Jid, the little beggar who was so attached to me. I was already looking forward to going home.

Despite being used to staying up till dawn, I fell asleep early. I woke up several times during the night, sensing in the air, in the cloudless sky, in the stars shining above me, some heavy presence, unknown and unreal. A formless anxiety crouched in my stomach. I looked around, trying to understand, and realised it was the silence that oppressed me. There was no noise at all: everyone was asleep, there were no car engines. Absolute peace. I'd never experienced anything like it.

When I opened my eyes, I saw a tablecloth spread in front of me with pieces of bread, a bowl of milk and some cheese on it. A young man was sitting nearby making tea.

He said, 'I'm Yacoub, Salma's nephew, your cousin if you like. Salma goes to the mosque very early for dawn prayers. She wanted you to rest a little.'

He had hair that fell to the nape of his neck, a round face with laughing eyes and a strong, determined chin. He was wearing a white shirt of dubious cleanliness and faded jeans with no apparent rips in them. I asked him to turn round so I could get out of my sheets. I was used to a leisurely morning toilette, but this time I just splashed my face with a little water and ran a brush through my hair. I didn't dare take my make-up out of my bag: it seemed inappropriate at a time of mourning, in a village with codes that were already beginning to weigh on me. I decided I would leave that day.

Yacoub began to talk about my mother. She was a gentle

woman, he said, who liked a quiet life of work and prayer. She and Salma raised goats in a pen behind the fields. They made butter, henna and incense, and also cultivated a plot of land when the rains came. He told me about the sheikh, whom he worshipped, 'a man born and bred in purity, a heavenly soul', no less.

'I find it astonishing,' I said, 'to see a young man like you so committed to a religious sect.'

'It's not a sect,' he replied, smiling at my ignorance, 'it's just a large community of people who have a higher calling.'

'I don't quite understand this "higher calling".'

'Going beyond oneself.'

'I still don't understand, my friend, and I never will. I'm a woman who long ago chose life.'

'We love life here too. We love to work, we love to pray, we love our families, we love our sheikh.'

'Is he the absolute leader?'

'No, first and foremost he's the one with the *baraka*.'

'What *baraka*?'

'A divine gift, if you like.'

'What does that mean, a divine gift?' I asked, genuinely confused.

Yacoub laughed, which irritated me even more. I said, 'Listen, young man, maybe I don't know about these things—'

'Don't get angry,' he interrupted, 'it's just that I don't want to bore you with "these things", as you call them. Especially as you're dealing with a bereavement.'

I was silent for a moment, then decided to confront him; certainties have always annoyed me.

'You're young, but you're already stifling yourself: no

flirting, no music, no poetry, no real reading…'

Yacoub laughed again. 'Oh no, you think I'm a savage? I've got girlfriends, I know music and I listen to it when I'm alone. I know about literature. I love poetry.'

'You've studied?'

'Modern literature at the university. I'm a student on holiday. A holiday that's been going on for a year now and is still going on.' He laughed.

'So what kind of poetry do you like?'

'All of it. Would you like me to recite some?'

'Do you know any of our poetry, from here?'

'Of course! Listen to these beautiful lines:

My beloved, how could you have dared to think
For one moment that all these trials
The distance, the thorns, the downpours, the beasts,
the dark of the night
Could have held me back?
Nothing could keep me from you.'

'Those lines are by Sam!' I cried.

'How do you know that?'

'He's my best friend!'

'Well, he's a great poet, even if…'

'Ah yes! You mean he's not from Louad…'

We laughed together. I began to see Yacoub with new eyes. Salma's arrival cut our conversation short.

I was struck again by how nimble this blind woman was. She hardly used her acacia stick; it only served as an occasional support because of her weak leg. She set about sweeping the courtyard with a broom.

The women began to return and sing new funeral orations. I felt as if my chest was about to burst, my breathing to stop. I was oppressed by the atmosphere, the sensation of being enclosed, those soft voices penetrating my ears and my heart. I used the excuse of going to the toilet several times, shutting myself in for as long as possible to escape the commotion.

The voices fell silent when a tall black woman arrived. She wore a long dress in shimmering colours and a kerchief on her head. She was accompanied by a pale young woman who winked constantly and another, dressed in black, who kept her head bowed. 'That's the sheikh's mother, sister and wife,' Salma whispered in my ear. I stood up to welcome them. The sheikh's mother sat down next to me and said in a loud voice, 'I was very fond of your mother, she visited me often. She didn't speak much, but she was a good listener and she had a lovely laugh.' She had a pronounced foreign accent, which she didn't seem at all self-conscious of. I felt real compassion emanating from her. The other two women shook my hand, spoke words of condolence in hushed tones, then inserted themselves into the group and joined in the chorus. The sheikh's mother didn't chant, but continued speaking to me as if the context of mourning was irrelevant: 'Will you stay with us, my daughter?'

'No,' I replied, 'I'll go back to town after the condolences.'

'You're right, my girl, the town is a better place for a beautiful woman like you. You'll easily find a husband you like and you'll live happily ever after.'

She stood up, still squeezing my hand. 'You'll come back

to see me when all of this is over, won't you?' I nodded. Salma went to see her out. When she returned, she confided in me, 'The sheikh's mother never belonged to our path, but she's a kind woman with a big heart. Everyone loves her.'

At lunchtime, I refused to eat the pancakes soaked in lamb gravy that I'd always relished. I was counting the hours until evening, when the women would leave. When I couldn't hold out any longer, I whispered to Salma that I had to leave the house, to walk around the village and get some air. She tried to get me to wait, saying. 'But this is your mother's mourning!' I replied, 'Either I go out and catch my breath now, or I'll have to leave here for good.' Salma called a young girl and whispered something to her. The girl withdrew, came back a few minutes later and spoke softly to her. At last I was allowed to leave, but the route I had to take was mapped out for me.

'You must go and pray in front of your mother's tomb: the cemetery's not far away. Tomorrow you'll go and pay your respects to the sheikh and offer your condolences to him. Yes, that's how it is here. Despite his young age, the sheikh is the father of all of us, and our friend too. Your cousin Yacoub will accompany you.'

I left under the disapproving glances of the women. Yacoub was waiting for me outside the door. He was now wearing a large, well-pressed *boubou,* a clean white shirt from a cheap brand and sandals that looked new.

'Wow! You're looking good now!'

'We're expecting a delegation from the mayor.'

'The mayor? What's that thug doing here?'

'Talking to the sheikh about a government project. A dam.'

'A dam here would be great! Just looking around, the

need for it is obvious.'

'It's not going to happen. The sheikh is against it, and so are the rest of us.'

'But why?'

'We have enough water. We only work with our hands, never with those pumps that destroy the crops, and this land isn't meant for that kind of project. It's meant for prayer.'

He spoke in a sententious tone this time, looking towards the sheikh's house, where a few people were gathered outside the door. He seemed anxious.

'I'll never understand you people,' I said.

Yacoub didn't answer. He led me quickly towards the cemetery.

All the graves looked the same: a few stones surrounding a small mound of sand, a cement slab with the name of the deceased followed by a brief epitaph. First Yacoub stopped in front of two tombs that seemed to be those of the first sheikhs of the brotherhood, then I discovered, written in a clumsy hand, the name of my mother. I stopped. No, Mother, I thought, I won't live like you, bowing your whole life under the weight of misery, of a tyrannical husband, then of a faith that forbade you from living. You abandoned your loved-ones, two innocent little girls, to imprisonment by a father incapable of love. You did it because you were afraid, they said. Well I rejected fear and submissiveness. I said no. No man will ever tyrannise me, no faith or power will ever make me bow my head. I will obey only my heart and my impulses, I will seek only my own happiness, I will follow only my own will! Rest in peace, you who've known nothing but hardship. I, your daughter, will never become what you were.

SAARA

Yacoub urged me to leave. 'The visit to the fields can wait,' he said, 'I'm going to the meeting the sheikh has called. I'll see you at home later.' He almost ran. I decided I wasn't going back to that dull mourning room any time soon. Interminable laments were not for me; it had been too long since I cut ties with boredom, and this isolated little village was not going to reel me back in. My nostalgia for my mother wouldn't last forever. She was buried now. It was over. I'd cried for her, but I wouldn't lie down and die on her grave. I walked down Louad's only street, lost in my thoughts and emotions. I found myself near the assembly Yacoub had been talking about.

There wasn't much of an audience, just a few men. In the distance I saw the mayor, sitting behind an empty table, talking and waving his arms around. Moustaff the Horrible, as Sam called him, was up to his usual tricks—he must have smelled money in the air. Was he planning to buy all of Louad too? I remembered what Yacoub had said about a dam: of course Moustaff must have an interest in that. I approached a little closer and saw him frown slightly, surprised to see me there. Next to him was a young man wearing a light turban that fell to the nape of his neck. He had a well-trimmed beard, clear eyes that expressed a peaceful certitude and a round face that was calling for calm. The sheikh.

Moustaff spoke forcefully, as was his custom, pumping his fists in the air as he did during election campaigns, and using the same discourse: development, wealth, water, electricity, the president of the republic as protector of the nation... Moustaff always won, because of his powerful connections and his enormous fortune, not to mention the ballot-stuffing and corruption.

I almost shouted, 'Don't drink this corrupted water, vomit it up! It will turn bitter, it will rot your stomachs, it's all lies!' I kept quiet though, intimidated in spite of myself by the look the young sheikh was giving me from afar.

Moustaff finally fell silent and turned to the sheikh, gesturing at the crowd. 'Our mayor wanted to speak to you,' the sheikh said hesitantly, 'so I called you here today to listen to him. We thank him very much for his visit, and we will not forget him in our prayers.' The mayor didn't seem satisfied with these words. He waved his hand again, said something I couldn't hear, then got up quickly and went to his car. He didn't wait for the sheikh, who made to follow him. I saw Yacoub take the mayor by the arm, stop him for a few seconds and say some words that didn't seem pleasant. Moustaff shook Yacoub off, shouting expletives, and got into his large vehicle, which sped away. The sheikh went back into his house. I felt as if I'd been disobedient, trespassed into a world that didn't belong to me, witnessed a scene I wasn't supposed to see. I retraced my steps to get away, but a man came running towards me, the same person I'd met on my arrival. 'Come back,' he said, 'the sheikh would like to see you.'

The sheikh sat cross-legged on a thick woollen rug. Around him, a Babylonian confusion of cushions, mineral water bottles, milk cartons, half-empty glasses. Yacoub was beside him, his head bowed in shame.

'Welcome, sister,' said the sheikh, 'please excuse the mess; we've just had a visit from the mayor and we haven't had a chance to clear up. Take a seat next to your cousin.'

'I'm not sure if I should,' I said. 'He seems to be getting a telling off.'

'No, no, I was giving him some advice.'

'I know I was wrong to grab his arm, Sheikh,' said Yacoub, 'but I didn't say anything rude.'

'Didn't say anything rude? Please don't tell lies.'

'All I did was ask him to wait till you got up.'

'I heard everything!'

'Then I just added that he and all his offerings weren't worth a hair on your head.'

'Our path forbids vanity, Yacoub. We mustn't boast about ourselves, or anyone close to us.'

'I was just giving my opinion.'

'Your opinion is not a truth. It's not the truth. You have no worth in yourself, Yacoub. Nor do I: I'm just your brother who chance has made the head of this order. Only the path has value. And it tells us to respect authority. You owe the mayor your respect.'

I couldn't let that go. I said, 'Moustaff the Horrible deserves no-one's respect!'

The sheikh threw me a glance that was both serious and amused. Something inside me dissolved. It was as if his eyes were boring into me, his voice caressing me, his smile enveloping me whole.

'You have character, sister,' he said softly, 'but here we're not in the habit of denouncing our governors, whoever they may be.'

'Moustaff only governs for himself.'

'Perhaps, but he has the authority of having been elected.

Louad is just a tiny part of his jurisdiction. We won't enter into conflict with those in power; all we ask is that they let us practise our faith. But sister, I invited you here to offer my condolences. I should have gone to your mother's house, but the arrival of that official prevented me. Lalla was my mother too; she was Salma's cousin and friend, and Salma has always been like a mother to me.'

'I met your mother today,' I told him, 'you could say we hit it off.'

He smiled. 'My mother is from a different culture. She doesn't follow our path, she laughs at it in fact, but she's everything to me.'

'You're lucky to have a mother who loves you.'

I regretted the words as soon as I'd said them.

'Your mother loved you, I'm sure, and now the rest of us here love you too.'

At that moment a man presented himself. His clothes were ragged and he had a long beard. The sheikh signalled that Yacoub and I should leave and rushed over to greet him. As we walked out, the man averted his eyes, erasing me from his field of vision. I didn't exist for him.

'He's one of the followers of renunciation,' Yacoub explained when we got outside. 'They live up there. They've chosen a life of poverty, abstinence, prayer. They hardly ever come down from the mountain.'

'They've chosen death, then?'

'In a way.'

A shiver ran through my body.

The Sheikh

I left Louad and took my worries to walk on the forgotten trails of the old caravan routes. I refused company and went straight to where I'd arranged to meet the nomads. I told them I planned to stay with them for a few days, share a little of their lives. They made no reply, just glanced at each other, then carried on walking. I followed in their footsteps.

I was seeking a brief respite from the march of time, some breathing space in which I could try to decipher the complex scroll of my troubles. Storm clouds had gathered over Louad, but it was as if I'd been struck dumb: I struggled to name my own feelings, never mind offer a response to the hostile forces that threatened us.

The rude, boorish mayor had come, swaggering, to inform me that the dam would soon be built. Half of Louad would be razed to the ground. I was required to facilitate this hateful task and prepare our faithful for the managed death of our Medina. I explained that I could not accept our end, that for us it was not a question of space, time or material things, but only of faith. 'Louad,' I told the mayor, 'is the resting place of our hearts, bequeathed to us by my father and my grandfather. We chose it. We lit our fires and built our homes here. We planted our palm trees and our souls in this soil. Abandoning it would mean the end of our order.'

The mayor didn't listen. He waved his arms around, spoke of backwardness and fanaticism, then of progress and development. 'This land doesn't belong to you,' he said. 'No administration has ever granted it to you. The state has decided to build a dam here, and you're in no position to oppose it. The invitations to tender have been issued, the project manager has been chosen, and the equipment has already been ordered.' He then asked to speak directly to the residents of Louad. He thought it would be easy to convince them. I called some of them to us. He spouted the usual verbiage beloved of politicians, waxed lyrical about a future world of greenery and wealth. He thought he was in front of his usual audience, who probably nodded their heads at him without understanding a word. Our people made a show of listening, to please me, but they didn't believe his nonsense; all they expected from the dam was the collapse of our world. The mayor realised his approach wasn't going to work. He demanded I talk to them, make his point for him, though he already knew my opinion. When I offered nothing but polite phrases, he became enraged.

Then, just when I needed to draw on all the strength of spirit I had, a young woman from the slums of the new settlements came knocking on the door of my serenity. Everything about her attacked me: the way she walked towards us, the surprised look she gave me at first, the soft sparkle in her eyes, the hair she couldn't hide, the way part of her breast could be seen—unconscious on her part, but indecent, I admit—her voice when she finally spoke. She had none of the wisdom, the spirit of forgiveness or the humility that our path teaches. Instead she was strong and made sure to appear so; she refused the dictates of both spirit and reason. Abandoned at an early age, she'd developed a habit of independence detrimental to decorum and to faith. Despite all of that, I sensed her to be true. In any case, with no effort whatsoever at seduction, she'd profoundly shaken a tree I thought I'd planted firmly.

In Louad then, too many voices called out to me, too many possible responses suggested themselves. I'd heard no whisper of my saving instincts in my ears. Neither the holy books, nor the precepts of our path, nor my father's teachings had made any provision for this. I had no ammunition to oppose either the threat to our settlement or the brazen gaze of a girl from the city. I was afraid to open my hands and find them empty. The followers of renunciation had refused to give me any answers. 'The questions are in you and so are the answers,' they'd said, before returning to their prayers. I was lost.

To end this vacillation, to try to access my deeper awareness, I had to return to the space of truth, the place where the message of my forefathers had been born, where the followers of renunciation always said that everything began: the desert.

My time with the nomads did heal me a little. I rediscovered an order of things inside myself and savoured the deep calm that being in open spaces could bring. I subdued the unruly emotions that battled inside me and located my serenity. I lived with the camel-herders for a fortnight. They were illiterate, but they knew how to sense the approach of strong winds, smell distant rain and take the winding roads to the best pastures without getting lost. That alone taught me something. They knew all of this while I, the supreme sheikh of the best of all paths, with a whole brotherhood awaiting my instructions, was grappling blindly for a way forward. When I came into contact with those wide open spaces and those simple spirits, I understood what our ascetics meant: that every person had their own answer, and that it could only come from inside them, in its own time.

Only then was I able to inhale the perfume of time passing. I forgot the demands on me and just looked up at the sky, my mind empty, and experienced the infinite. I returned to the primordial dimension and realised that things never explained themselves; they needed to be interpreted. The nomad herders knew what the wind meant by blowing, what they sky meant by offering up rain or sunshine. I too had to learn to listen to my surroundings. I had to think like the nomads, chiefs of their realm, who never hesitated over which direction to take, how to get to the well, how to care for their camels. Without their knowledge, they would perish. They didn't try to understand life; they just lived it. I'd been surrounded by too many people; I was too highly-educated, too revered. I'd never learned how to walk.

So I followed, panting, in the trails of lost animals, then returned to my friends, who trotted more than they walked, so that I had to run to catch up with them. I experienced immense physical fatigue, and at times, profound confusion. But at the first stop, the tea tasted as precious as forbidden liqueurs, the stale dates like apples from Eden. The pieces of dried meat spread out on the white sand seemed to me like a pharaoh's banquet.

In the space of a few days, I began to notice the imprints of our elemental truths, to tune in to appeals to the ancient prophets echoing back from the vaults of time. I experienced no great revelations, but I understood that it was possible to take the right road without finding the right word for it, and that it might be necessary to live as a nomad for a long time before discovering peaceful terrain.

It was difficult to leave the desert. But Louad was calling me, and I had to answer.

I came back at night, while the oasis was sleeping. I went straight to my mother's tent and gently shook her awake.

'Sweet Mother…'

She raised wide, incredulous eyes to me. 'Oh my dear son!' She embraced me, weeping. 'I was frightened, child! I had no idea where you were! How could you let your poor mother worry like that?'

'Dearest Mother, I told you! I said I was going into the desert for a few days.'

'The desert is vast, child! You didn't tell me where exactly you were going.'

'I met incredible people there.'

'You look exhausted. Those shadows under your eyes, and my God, your face is all burned!'

'It's nothing.'

She woke a young servant and asked her to prepare tea

and a light meal.

'Tell me all about it, son.'

'There's nothing to tell. And everything. The silence, the emptiness, the exquisite taste of complete isolation. The exhaustion of the days, the joy of the evenings… everything, and nothing.'

'Ah, my son, your mother has terrible memories of that endless desert. Such hard months I spent there.'

'It is hard. And so beautiful.'

'It was never beautiful to me. I was so young. I came from a different world. I was afraid and alone, far from my people.'

'My father was with you!'

'Your father was with his prayers and his books. He was never with anyone, especially not me.'

I changed the subject: I didn't like it when she talked that way about my father. 'What did you do while I was gone?'

'Nothing. I saw Saara every day. The daughter of my dear departed friend Lalla.'

'Every day?'

'Yes. She's not boring like most of the women here.'

'Mother!'

'I'm sorry, son, but Saara thinks the same. Then there's that dam everyone's talking about.'

'What are your thoughts?'

'That she's very beautiful.'

'No, about the dam!'

'As far as I can see, it'll mean more water, more crops and more work.'

'The town will swallow us up, Mother! Our path could be swept away by hostile forces.'

'You're saying your path can't stand up to a dam?'

'It's not that. It'll bring new people, new powers. A new world.'

'Ah. And is it not possible that this new world might bring some happiness?'

'What an idea, Mother! That world is all ignorance and vulgarity. What it will do is consume us.'

'Don't get angry, son.'

'Forgive me. In any case, they're not giving us a choice.'

'Yes, God can match every hostile force with another.'

'Oh, Mother.'

'I don't mean to speak badly of your faith.'

'Can it really be possible that after so many years, you still can't follow the path of my father, your dead husband?'

'Your father was my master, child. I belonged to him. I was his possession. No one ever asked me what I thought.'

'But you were the companion of the Great Sheikh! Something all the women of the Sahara dream of!'

'Is that so? And what makes you think I share the dreams of all the women of the Sahara?'

'Please forgive me, Mother, but my father was a great scholar and a saint.'

'Is that any concern of mine? He gave me you. That's enough.'

'Oh Mother!'

Conversations with my mother were often like this when they got round to our tribe or our order. Deep down, she'd never accepted either. Louad was still the enemy, the place that had made a prison of her youth. Even though the people of the oasis had learned to respect and even love her, my mother stubbornly refused to bow to her conquerors. Her kohl-lined eyes shone with nostalgia for some distant time and place. She remained faithful to this unknown past, and to words that had no meaning for us. I sometimes felt angry that I didn't know her better, that I was ignorant about her childhood or her former sufferings, but she said, 'What's the point of knowing about that? Your birth erased it all. You're my world now; you're my new life, my only life.' I couldn't think of a response to that. I just liked to be with her, to bask in her love. She was the only person for whom I was not the sheikh. She didn't care about an idea, or an order, or a turban, just about me.

The next day, from dawn prayers onwards, everyone in Louad came to kiss my hand and thank God for my return. I sensed fear in all of them. The people of our brotherhood could see the clouds gathering above them, heralding a change in the weather, but they didn't know if it would mean welcome rain for the crops or a flood that would wash the fields away. I also heard some upsetting news. While I was away, policemen had come and arrested Yacoub. The mayor had accused him of assault, when it was he who had attacked a pious and peaceful community. Mohand had also returned.

Mohand was my first cousin. His father was my father's elder brother, and was known for his great erudition, as well as—this was only said in a whisper—his pride. When my grandfather died, my uncle naturally sought to claim the turban of the path, but the followers of renunciation rejected him in favour of my father. Though my father was younger and less scholarly, they considered him more pious. My uncle retired to his tent until his death, keeping silent, praying, and some say, brooding over this rejection.

Mohand and I had grown up together, played and studied together. We often competed in our recitations and our attempts to charm the young virgins of Louad. A certain mistrust had developed between us, but I never imagined it could turn into blind animosity on his part. Despite our differences, and despite the disdain many of the faithful had for him, I always considered Mohand a good follower of the path, as well as a friend. He was intelligent, pragmatic and had better knowledge of the outside world than I did. But as soon as we became adults, he showed the strongest aversion to me. He even tried to create a schism in our order by seeking recognition from some of our followers for himself. He didn't succeed. He went into exile and disappeared somewhere in the jungle of the new cities. We heard little more about him.

I didn't see Saara during the procession of the faithful. All the women of Louad passed in front of me, bowing their heads and praying for my happiness and that of our oasis, but Saara wasn't among them. Had she gone back to the city? Should I rejoice at her absence? I kept Salma talking for a while, but she didn't mention Saara and I didn't dare ask.

After all the faithful had left, José came to see me. He visited me every Sunday after the first prayers. We'd eat breakfast together and talk at length. José didn't believe in anything; not in God, not in saints, not in ideologies. He believed, he said, only in human beings and their weaknesses, and in medicine. I'd say to him, 'José, you don't like ideologies, you don't like religions, but it's clear from listening to you that you don't know anything about ideologies or religions; you only know about the science of the visible!'

'And you, Qotb, head of a medieval brotherhood in a remote village, you know nothing about science or the modern world—you're from another time!'

Our altercations invariably ended in laughter. But more often than not, we discussed local affairs: the sick people; the treatments they needed; the medical evacuations that sometimes had to be carried out. On this particular day, José was sullen. 'In Atar, I was summoned by the mayor,' he told me.

'What for?'

'He asked about you, what our relationship was, why I came here. I told him I was a doctor, that I didn't work for him but for the state, as part of the agreement it has with my country, that I was free on my days off, and that you were my friend.'

'What did he want to know about our relationship?'

'He seemed to suspect some dark conspiracy, something underhand between your brotherhood and me.'

'Bad people see bad in everything.'

'Yes, but the truth is he's also a coward. He wanted to make sure you didn't have any powerful foreign supporters. And that's precisely what worries me.'

'Why is that worrying?'

'It means he's looking for a confrontation. He also mentioned your cousin.'

'Mohand?'

'Yes. He said he'd had a visit from him, that he was an educated, modern man, and that he had more legitimacy than you to lead the brotherhood.'

'Mohand left Louad of his own volition. He came back during my absence, but he hasn't visited me yet, even though it's the tradition.'

'I understand Mohand asked the prefect to banish you. He's saying everywhere that you're stirring up dissent.'

'I don't care about Mohand and his treachery! No one will believe his lies. It's only this dam that worries me. Do you think they'll build it anyway?'

'Yes, and I'll tell you why. Because it's in the mayor's interest. The whole administration is in his pocket, the prefect most of all, and he'll use him to put pressure on you.'

'The dam will be the death of our brotherhood.'

'I don't see it that way. In principle, I'm in favour of dams. Even if I know what the deal is with this one.'

'Which is?'

'The mayor's company will partly construct it, then after it's built, he'll seize several plots of land and distribute others to his friends. You'll be expelled, and they'll recruit a mass of underpaid workers who they can lay off in drought years.'

'What can we do?'

'Strongly oppose it.'

'We're already doing that.'

'Through prayers?'

'Yes, prayers, and words.'

'That will never be enough.'

'We have no other means. I know what you're thinking, José. You believe in big demonstrations, shows of force, the resistance you call legitimate. All of that would be impossible for us—we're an order dedicated to God. We reject all violence, because we believe that it's heresy, that it distances us from the divine.'

José left, railing against our fatalism and inertia. But there was nothing I could do. I was bound by the oaths of my father and my grandfather to make Louad a place where hatred or exclusion could never grow, where violence was banned, where the only passion expressed was for our faith.

As soon as José left, a stranger was announced. I got up quickly to greet a young man dressed in a light, immaculate white *boubou* and a short black shirt. He had a turban around his neck and his hair was dishevelled. His eyes sparkled with intelligence and also, it was immediately obvious, with irony. He introduced himself simply as Sam. The poet, I'd heard of him. What was a poet of pleasure doing in Louad?

I invited him to sit. 'Welcome to the land of the ascetics. I don't yet want to know why you've come to us. We're honoured by your presence.'

'I won't stay long.'

'You'll have lunch with us, then you're free to stay or to leave.'

'I've just come to see how a dear friend of mine is doing, then I'll be on my way.'

'You'll have lunch with the ascetics. Don't worry, it won't kill you. It's just a tradition that old-fashioned people like us try to keep alive. I can tell you that your friend is doing fine.'

'Saara?'

'She's the only person here who a great poet could know.'

'She said she was only leaving for a few hours, then she didn't come back. I was worried. I wanted to see her, but I was told I had to come and see you first.'

'Yes, that's also the tradition in Louad: any stranger who

passes through is first the guest of the sheikh.'

'I almost turned straight back around again.'

'Why? Are you afraid of me?'

'A little,' he said, laughing. 'I've heard that *marabouts* are no friends of poets.'

'But what isn't often said is that it's poets who refuse the friendship of *marabouts*. I'd be happy to be a poet's friend, if the poet would accept the outstretched hand of a man of God.'

'I know about the poetry that dwells in you Sufis.'

'A beautiful tribute from a man like you.'

'A glutton, a prevaricator of spirits, a servant of Satan…'

'I've never thought that!'

'Some of your followers would call me all of those things.'

'Many of our faithful only see the bark of our faith; they forget its roots.'

'I respect your path, I often envy your passion, but I love life too much.'

'I respect your choice, and in Louad you must respect ours.'

'I know. Could I see Saara, make sure she's in good health, and then leave?'

'You'll see her straight away, right here, because this is the only place in Louad where you can meet, but you won't be leaving immediately, I'm going to hold you back. We can't let an important poet get away so quickly.'

So I organised lunch, to which I invited Saara and José.

When Saara appeared, Sam jumped up to welcome her. Respectful of Louad's customs, they didn't kiss. I realised immediately that there was no love between them, only strong friendship. My heart ached when I saw her again: I realised

I'd made a mistake in inviting her; it was going to stir up the embers again. But what else could I have done? I couldn't let Sam go without granting him his interview, and it could only take place in my presence, in my house.

José came in singing, to provoke me a little. He cried, 'I'm bringing music to this valley of tears which forbids it!' I laughed at the theatrical voice he was using. 'That's some horrific braying you're bringing us, José,' I said.

I tried not to look at Saara during lunch. But it was impossible to escape her voice, the scent of her presence. She didn't speak much, and hardly ate at all. She gave brief answers to José's questions. Sam discussed poetry with José, and translated some of his own poems for him. Saara intervened once in this discussion, and I realised she knew about literature too. I removed myself from their conversation by reading a book and going often to the kitchens to check on the food. If I stayed in the room, I feared I'd give myself away. The presence of Saara was deeply disturbing to me, and I didn't want to start behaving like some would-be suitor. That would amount to a flouting of the teachings of our path. José left soon; he had patients waiting. Sam's head was starting to nod after his long, rough journey. Just before leaving, Saara addressed me. She wanted news of her cousin Yacoub. I replied that I had none.

'Why is it,' she asked, 'that no one here is interested in his fate, not even the sheikh, not even his aunt?'

'We all love him,' I said.

'What kind of love is that? No one's been to see what he's going through!'

'We have no fear for him.'

'I'll never understand you people,' she said, as she stood up. 'I'll go to Atar tomorrow and check on him.'

'Yacoub is a follower of our path. We're his only family, and his fate concerns us alone.'

'I'll be leaving tomorrow anyway. Salma wanted me to wait for your return.'

'And my blessing, she almost certainly added.'

'And your blessing, but I don't think you're likely to bless a frivolous woman like me.'

'Never let yourself be judged. We don't judge anyone here. You must stay with us a little longer.'

But what order could I give her? She was not of our path, and she obeyed no one.

Saara left without replying. I found myself instinctively reaching a hand into the empty air, as if to pull her back. I took a few steps forward, hoping she'd turn round, but she continued walking; slowly, majestically, without changing her pace. An enormous anxiety gripped me; the fear of letting something momentous escape, and also the fear of losing a part of myself.

That evening, after prayers, we had a session of *dhikr*, the raising of our voices to heaven to sing the melodies of our faith. We offered up our mortal weaknesses to the Mighty One, and recited poems of love written by my grandfather, the creator of the path. We repeated God's name thousands of times and sang the praises of his prophet and beloved. The congregation, borne away on the wings of faith, fell into ecstasy. Some began to dance and gesticulate, others wept profusely. I was moved. For those hours, I felt euphoria and forgot my torments.

When I returned to the world of appearances, I went to see

my mother, because I was afraid of Saara and of myself.

It was as if she'd been waiting for me, despite the late hour. She welcomed me with open arms. We embraced, and she started to sing some of the songs of my childhood. They had words I'd never understood, but which I sensed were sweet. I didn't talk to her about Louad or the path. I told her I saw Saara when I closed my eyes. My mother laughed. She said the heart knew no shores, that Saara was beautiful and that there was no harm in dreaming about her. 'But,' I said, 'she's a woman from a different place.'

'Your father,' she said, 'was also tripped up by the eyes and the body of a woman from a different place, but that one was a slave, and she wasn't happy until her son was born. Saara has charm. She's intelligent, generous, free. She's like me. She'll never belong to your father's path.'

'That's why,' I said, 'she could never belong to me. She's on the other side. The side of life.'

My mother laughed again. 'Who knows? Women are a deep sea, my son. They can hold anything in their arms, if it's for love!' Then she changed the subject to Mahjouba, my wife. 'She's a good wife, and she's expecting a child.' I didn't know what to say to that. I knew Mahjouba was a good woman, that she was pious, that she was expecting a child and that she was committed to the path. But nothing about her called out to me any more.

We stopped talking after that. I dozed, my mother sang softly and stroked my head. I mused to myself that she hadn't noticed me grow up, that in her eyes I was still a child. I laughed at the thought, and relief washed through my body and mind.

THE BEGGAR

Things felt wrong. The faces around me were blank: no smiles, no pity, no sneers, no frowns. People looked through me as though I was a stone, a wall, the air flowing past them. I was the dumb beggar, part of the scenery; they didn't object to me; I was just there. I wondered whether any of these people even looked at the stars any more. Probably they were conscious of nothing but the rumbling of their bellies. Behind their empty eyes I saw ugliness, and lives that were faded and broken. I still came down from the mountain every day, my pack on my back, to walk amongst that ugliness. I held out my hand, lowered my head, accepted the coins, the pieces of bread, the handfuls of sugar. Perhaps it made them feel as if they were showing their good side. I knew they had no good side.

For two days, I couldn't leave the house: my mother's suffering was too extreme. I sat with her through the night, stroked her temples, massaged her arms and legs, sang her some of Sam's poems. Yes, the mute beggar sang to his deaf mother. He also promised her that as soon as she was feeling better they'd leave, go to a city where no one knew them; he'd stop being a tramp scrabbling for leftovers, she'd stop being a deaf and dumb woman who lived up a mountain with a bastard child who'd inherited her afflictions. I told her I'd get a job, we'd have a house, with a roof and windows and a ceiling. I'd recover the voice they stole from me, perhaps I'd even find a wife and have some children. I'd teach my children to love her. I told my mother all sorts of things, my wishes and hopes, old ones and new. I uncorked my throat and spouted out all my impossible imaginings. Of course I knew I'd never escape my beggar's life. Still, it felt good to say those things.

After a while her suffering subsided; there were no more strangled breaths, no more whimpers. Her pain left her, her body began to loosen a little more with every hour. She was starting to move beyond time, to a place where I couldn't reach her. Exhausted from her struggle, she sank into lethargy. Perhaps the illness had weakened its grip, and her body and her spirit had been released, to float, motionless, just above her bed. I found myself elsewhere too. I felt as if I was wrapped in fog. At my centre was nothing. My joints were stiff and wouldn't co-operate. It was time for me to leave, but I didn't want to go out and walk those streets. I didn't want to hear the sounds of that marketplace. I didn't want to see the ugly faces of soulless citizens. But I had to go.

Up on the mountainside we were protected: the kids never ventured that far anymore, no one passed by; they all thought it was haunted. Even the noises of the town were subdued by the time they reached us. My mother and I enjoyed our peace: the scents of morning, the lullabies chanted by the wind. We felt the sun rising over our heads and we saw it slipping slowly into sleep. I took my mother outside to witness these marvels. She'd become blind, but the sleepy sun rays still spoke to her, and she still knew their language.

It was time to wake my mother, wash her, wrap her in the white sheet I'd cleaned while she was asleep, and leave beside it the new veil Saara had given me for her. My mother would put it on when she woke up; she never undressed in my presence. When I came back that evening, I'd try to get her to walk a bit. I'd tell her stories and make sure she ate. There was a pot of barley porridge ready-prepared, some bread that had already gone mouldy that I'd sprinkle with drops of tea. I'd get her to drink the whole teapot-full to give her strength. The rest of the leftover food I'd brought back from the city was useless now and starting to smell. My mother hardly ate any of it any more anyway. She had clean water, and two bottles of milk beside her, so she wouldn't have to drag herself up to drink. Later, I'd tell her more stories that she wouldn't hear, I'd sing for myself and for her, I'd dance, and maybe she'd feel it all, and maybe she'd smile, and I'd imagine she was happy. Perhaps we'd both think we were happy.

From our hut clinging to the side of the mountain, I could see the city and even beyond it. I imagined my mother falling asleep sheltered and cradled by the valley. It thought itself big, it liked to puff out its chest, but from my vantage point I could see it was tiny. I knew it was fragile too, that its bones were as tired as my mother's. I knew the oasis had grown too large. I knew about the illnesses that plagued it, the uncertainties that gnawed at it. I felt no pity for the city: it deserved to feel fear because it was stupid and vain.

The mountainside seemed steeper that day. Maybe it didn't know it was me: the previous two days had made me forget life; perhaps life had forgotten me too. When I saw Mama, she'd soon remind me of the city's rhythms. She'd tell me, in that whining voice of hers, about everything she'd seen, heard, felt, every tiny detail of her pathetic existence. She thought this information was getting through to me, that there was some secret thread that linked her world to mine. She was an idiot. I'd see the other beggars too, and the streets, and Saara and Sam. Maybe they'd thought about me sometimes. Sam once said to me, 'Stop begging, come and live with me. I live alone. You can bring your mother if you like.' I decided he must be crazy. Saara nodded, said, 'I'll help you and your mother too.' Both of them were crazy. They didn't know that to become a beggar was to remain a beggar: after it had happened to you, you couldn't live any other way. And what was the difference, a beggar to some people or a beggar to everyone? Had Saara and Sam guessed my secret? I didn't think so. Suddenly I was singing and running. I felt like shouting, talking, expressing joy and truth, just for a moment, before I set foot in the land of pretence.

I stopped at the crossroads; Zaza wasn't there. Zaza was a tough black man with flashing eyes and iron fists. He was tiny in fact, a midget, and he limped badly, but his powerful arms could choke you with one squeeze. His way of addressing the other beggars was to shout abuse and wave his fists at them. No one could get in front of him when a car stopped or a passer-by reached out a hand. I always tried to avoid him. Mama taunted him, even insulted him when he threatened me. He'd back away from her, smile when she attacked him. Was he in love with her? Did he even have emotions? I imagined a romance between Zaza and Mama: her with her round, silly face and her rheumy eyes, him with his premature wrinkles. It was impossible, it would be too grotesque.

I gave up at the crossroads and headed for the Central Market. I always stopped in front of Baba's restaurant. He was there with his friends; they were sitting on chairs, facing the main square, talking and smoking. All they did all day long was talk, smoke and drink tea. I knew them all. Sam greeted me with a big slap on the back. It hurt and I didn't appreciate it. I didn't want the others thinking I was his friend; I was just a beggar after all. Mahmoud was there: he loved books; he was always carrying one with him. He worked at the prefecture but he never went there. There was also Chabi, who was 'in business' and was married to Salma, who ran a hairdressing salon, and Hamed. I didn't know what Hamed did, but he knew Saara well too, I'd seen him at her place. Sometimes they were joined by other men from the town. I liked listening to them. They talked about mysterious worlds I couldn't imagine: faraway countries, aeroplanes, murders... the word 'politics' came up a lot, and they often said bad things about the mayor and the prefect. There was nothing they were afraid to say. That gave me the shivers. Sam also recited poems, which I found beautiful. I hung on every word. I wondered whether I might recite a poem one day, when I dared to speak again. Why speak unless it was to say beautiful things? Sometimes I felt an urge to repeat those beautiful words out loud, but that would have been impossible—I was deaf and dumb. If Mama wasn't clinging to my back, I'd wait for the glass of tea Baba offered me and the coin he gave me every day, stroking my head, saying, 'Off you go, little one…'

Mama usually caught up with me in front of the vegetable seller. She'd show me what she'd earned: a few coins, dates, lumps of sugar, sometimes a note. I'd warned her plenty of times, I'd shaken my head and waved my hands, almost growled, 'No' from the back of my throat, opened my eyes wide, but she didn't want to understand. She took the notes from people when I wasn't there and laughed at what she thought was a windfall, but I knew it was a bad idea to take that much from people. Beyond a few small crumbs it was no longer charity, but a debt you might have to pay back one day, with your body or your heart. I knew people, I listened to them, and I knew it wasn't goodness that inhabited the universe. I knew that Hamou, so pious and respected, was a sadist who oppressed his staff and beat his wife and children. I knew that Mini, the cloth merchant, had almost killed Massoud, the taxi driver, when he found him with his wife. He broke his tooth, but it was just between them, a fight for their honour. I knew a lot of things, because I was deaf and dumb and nobody paid any attention to me.

There were only a few people in the world, like Saara and Sam, who could be trusted. What hurt the most, what made it almost impossible for me to stop myself from screaming, was when they talked about my mother. They said she had a bastard son, that her own people had sent her away, that she stole me and I became a deaf-mute because I stayed with her for so long. They claimed she'd led a dissolute youth, that she'd cheated on a great *marabout* and God had punished her. I moved away quickly when I heard them talking like that, in case I aroused suspicion. If I stayed, I might burst, and throw all their 'truths' back in their faces.

Apart from Mama, only Lamine knew I could talk. He was a boy of about my age. He walked on crutches, but he was agile, and when he sang out, 'Charity, charity, God will repay you!' his voice broke the hearts of old ladies. Sometimes, when it was too hot and there were very few passers-by, he and I would sit under a tree and play cards. We shared our meals, but he never stopped saying bad things about Saara, talking rubbish, adding signs so I could understand him. I used to just shake my head to let him know it wasn't true, but one day, when it was only the two of us, he went too far. I grabbed his dirty shirt, tripped him so he fell over, then stamped on him for a long time, shouting, 'This is for Saara, you dirty beggar!' He was so shocked he didn't even cry. We didn't speak after that. He moved away quickly whenever I came near him. When I wasn't around, he told everyone I was neither deaf nor dumb. Fortunately they didn't believe him.

Saara's house was very big, with a wide courtyard with a palm tree in the centre. There was a huge veranda, an enormous living room, and stairs leading to a room upstairs, where only Saara and her friends could go. I'd sit in the shade of the palm tree or on my mat and wait. I never went into the rooms, always refused Saara's invitations. There was a barrier, like a thick black line, between me and everyone else, even Saara. Beyond that wall was a world that wasn't for me and would never accept me. It was dark in there and I wouldn't be able to see things properly. I wouldn't know the right gestures, my words would be dead inside me, my feet would be ashamed to walk on the carpets, even though they were threadbare. I was a stranger in the kingdom of normal people. Saara kept inviting me in, because she couldn't see the force field of fear that stopped me from stepping forward. Sometimes she came and talked to me under the palm tree. I think she almost forgot she was talking to a deaf person. She looked me straight in the eye, enunciated her words slowly, made gestures to indicate her heart, her breasts, her stomach, touched her cheek, pointed to the sky. I was transfixed by these mimes. I forgot the meaning of the words, I was so captivated by the grace of Saara's movements. She asked about my mother. I told her she was ill, demonstrated with my hand under my head that she was confined to bed. I grimaced to show that it hurt, put my hand over my heart to say I was worried and I loved my mother very much. Saara was moved; I saw tears in her eyes. That wasn't what I wanted, so I indicated tomorrow with my finger pointing to the sky and told her my mother would get up again, would find life again—that meant begging again—and that then I'd become a football player and we'd both travel far away. The sound of an aeroplane was easy for my lips. Saara laughed and hugged me. I could smell her perfume.

I did love watching children play football. I envied them running, screaming, falling over, getting angry, crying and laughing. I'd get so caught up in watching them, I'd forget to go and beg. I'd have to stop myself shouting, 'Goal!' or 'Foul!' The kids often chased me away. I'd leave for a while, then come back. Once there was no one to play in goal, so Mourad, a gangly kid with ears like a squirrel's, said, 'The beggar! Let's try the beggar, while we're waiting.' The others laughed at first, then agreed. They played on a half-pitch, with just one goal. My God, how I leapt into the air and dived to the ground. I did well; both teams were encouraging me, even applauding. But when the game was over, the kids got changed, splashed water on their faces and went home without a backward glance. Things and people returned to their places. I was the deaf-mute beggar, son of the deaf-mute beggar, again. They'd drawn the curtain back across, so I couldn't see the shadows of other lives moving around without me. Still, those brief moments planted pleasure in me that reawakened every time I thought about that day. Sometimes I had dreams in which I was a child like any other, in a family like any other, and was a good football player, cheered on by a crowd. Then my mother's moans would bring me back to reality.

There was something wrong in the world. Sometimes I thought it must be the devil who ruled in the city, not God. Maybe He'd left, outraged by the injustice and deception, angry at the people of the place and at the whole of mankind. Maybe He'd abandoned us all, including my mother and me, both of us crippled by life. I told my mother not to worry, that one day He'd remember us again and come to our rescue. My mother's thoughts were written all over her face. She wanted to know when. I told her I couldn't say, but we had to tell ourselves the day would come, otherwise we'd sink into the swamp of despair. There was always a star speaking somewhere, asking to be looked at, to be loved.

Sometimes I felt so tired. My limbs ached from walking, my head was empty from forgetting so much, my stomach was hollow, my heart was sad. I'd sit down in the shade of a wall, and I'd feel like running away from this world that didn't want me. Why did I exist, I asked myself, what was it in me that called out to be alive? And then I'd find it. It was love. I loved my mother and I loved Saara. There was also him. I hated him. He'd left me stained, stolen my body and my mind. The next day, or the day after, or in a month, or a year, or a century, he'd pay. I'd get up then, because I'd found love and hate again, which meant I'd found life.

One day I got to Saara's house and found the front door locked. I couldn't believe it. That door was worm-eaten from standing open all morning, all afternoon, even all night. There were always people, even when Saara was upstairs in her bedroom, sleeping or entertaining friends. There was always me, and the poet, and his friends, and the singer. Something must have happened, something huge. An overwhelming fear gripped me; my whole body started to shake. I looked around. There was no one in the little alley, so I ran towards the shop on the corner. I almost let my voice out in a scream, but I held myself back at the last moment. With all my strength, I made a sound at the back of my throat. The shop keeper wasn't happy either: Saara and her friends were his best customers. He made agitated gestures with his hands. I didn't understand until he accompanied them with words: 'Saara has gone beyond the mountain, to Louad. Her mother is dying.' I had no idea Saara had a mother too. I looked down to see Saara's little cat brushing against my ankles, looking for her scent. I picked it up.

I thought about it for a while, weighing up the pros and cons: my mother, Saara... I decided Louad wasn't too far, it was only on the other side of the mountain. I'd go and take the little cat to Saara. Mama could look after my mother: cook for her, wash her, talk to her, smile at her. She knew how to do that.

SAARA

The sullen heaviness of the weather, my relentless internal interrogations, the feeling that Louad was distant and Atar hostile, my friends who were either too present or too absent, the mourning that sat so awkwardly on me, the tugging at my heart that I studiously ignored, the ache I couldn't place. All of those things conspired to steal my days and nights from me.

I counted the hours as they passed, yet I expected nothing. The revels broke out as usual every evening in my house, but something inside me had died: the music, the laughter, the shouts of joy from my friends, all landed like punches on my exhausted body. A listlessness had taken up residence in me. I had moments of sudden fear that I'd be trapped in that state forever. I ached for my youth and for my dreams; the ones I'd always kept quiet but had never completely buried.

Yet there was something else inside me too: a force calling on me to resist, to remain the person who'd always laughed in the face of misery and boredom. Outwardly, I expressed cheerfulness, in case that persuaded me into a good mood. I pulled on the clothes of happiness, though they couldn't cover me completely. It didn't work. I smiled while continuing to feel a deep, dragging emptiness.

I tortured myself with the thought that I'd missed out on everything I could have had. I'd kept on waiting for my mother when it was she who was waiting for me. Instead of going to look for her, I'd tried to forget her. I could have been loved every day, but instead I'd let my mother remain lost to me for all those years because I was blinded by spite, by the rage of believing myself abandoned, by ignorance of the kind of person she'd become; when I had no idea what kind of person I was either.

My feelings for the sheikh were the hallucinations of a heart that had lost its way: a hopeless, deluded, perversely persistent passion. I could not remain a prisoner to such an absurd derangement of the senses. I was Saara, a woman with loose morals and a free spirit, and he was Qotb, the leader of a brotherhood from another era, the *imam* of a faith that rejected the joys of the body and dreamed of an afterlife! Two such opposing planets could never be reconciled.

Who was left, then, for me to love? Only my little sister, and she'd fled without so much as a backward glance, oblivious to my despair. I'd always called that betrayal, but I began to wonder whether a loving heart shouldn't be open to forgiveness. Perhaps my sister had just loved me so much she couldn't bear to witness my grief.

I didn't know what to think, and I couldn't stop brooding on the past. What had happened to prevent her from ever calling or sending a letter? My stomach clenched. What if she was in trouble, abandoned, ill? What if she was ashamed to come back and was waiting for me to contact her? Who was she confiding in? Why had I let go of the one love that might still be available to me?

As soon as I'd had this thought, I couldn't wait: I decided I needed to retrace her journey, to sniff out every inch of sand she'd crossed, to climb the mountains she'd climbed, to know. I no longer felt I could live without knowing.

Sam said nothing. He understood my reasons but had no advice to give. That was the way he was: he never knew which side to take because for him all sides were equal and everyone had to feel their own way. Aziza encouraged me to leave. Zeinab thought I should forget an ungrateful sister who'd abandoned me. She was tough, never pulled her punches. Cheibou and the others said a little trip wouldn't do me any harm.

Though I loathed the place, I decided to start my search in the capital. Aziza had a sister, Gallia, who lived there. She was married to some important man. 'You'll see,' Aziza told me, 'they're unbelievably boring, but Gallia loves me. They'll both try to help us. I must go with you.' I agreed. Aziza was crazy, but I loved her company. She talked non-stop, jumping from one subject to another, and her voice was like music. She was skinny, with small, sparkling eyes and a well-defined mouth that was always smiling. She loved to sing and dance. Men liked Aziza, but she was too fickle to keep just one: every day she fell in love, every day she left a lover behind. She did often say that things could have lasted with Sam, but Sam was another story.

Cheibou wanted to come with us. We called him 'our fag'. When we first met him, he'd been ashamed of his nature, but Aziza shouted, 'Hey, faggot!' at him so much that finally he came out. Like Aziza, he loved to dance, but above all he loved to play the guitar. His dream was to go to the capital, study and become a great guitarist. Cheibou was very nice, but he was also very talkative. Sometimes I had to shut him up. Sam was the only one who really listened to him and believed in his talent.

I dissuaded Sam from coming. I knew he loathed the uncaring city, the home of his family and his most unpleasant memories. I also knew that if he did come, Aziza would spend the whole time clinging to him, trying for the umpteenth time to win him back, and would get distracted from helping me. I hadn't seen the little beggar for a few days, and Sam said he hadn't bumped into him either. Was his mother still ill? I didn't have time to find out, but Sam promised he'd check on her.

There was no chance of getting bored during the journey: my fellow travellers never stopped singing, telling jokes and bickering. They called each other 'dirty faggot' and 'naughty bitch' all the way, laughing immediately after insulting each other. I did all the driving: Cheibou couldn't drive and Aziza was too addicted to speed. The five hundred kilometres we had to cover were largely desert, the landscape monotonous and barren, sometimes lightly strewn with stunted plants, desert pavement and stones. The tarmac, a long, unchanging, straight black strip, disappeared into the blazing sun.

The only town we passed through, Akjoujt, was sleeping already, felled by an afternoon of scorching heat. First a colonial fort, then a mining town, dead before it could come alive again, the place seemed to have survived the slump, even if its best years were unmistakably over.

We stopped at Asma, a village that had once attempted to sneak land from the desert and become a city, but had long since accepted defeat. Our innkeeper, a middle-aged woman, received us wide-eyed. She offered us mint tea and a bowl of camel's milk. I dozed off for a bit and heard her whispering in Cheibou's ear, 'Why is she doing the driving on such a long journey? It's not normal for a woman!' and Cheibou replying, 'She looks like a woman, but there's a man hiding inside her. I'm the opposite.' The innkeeper quickly withdrew, scandalised. Aziza burst out laughing, chasing away my sleep.

Finally, Nouakchott greeted us with its ostentatious lights, its many vehicles—all either too old or too new—its dusty avenues, its lifeless crowds, its vain boutiques, the sand of its streets, the insolence of its looks and the inscrutability of its smiles. I said to Aziza, 'If it wasn't for my sister, I'd never have come to this place.' I hated our modern cities, fresh out of the dunes and so pleased with themselves. Atar had slipped through several centuries as a small oasis town, a caravan stopover and a colonial fort, before half-heartedly claiming the title of city. It had managed to preserve a remnant of its character, some of its past, a certain way of being that was very much its own and was shared by a good part of its inhabitants. Nouakchott, on the other hand, had no soul. Large numbers of people from elsewhere were born and lived there, but never claimed to be of the place. It was a city that nobody liked because it liked nobody. It was true you could meet every possible kind of person there: nomads still inhabited by their Sahara, villagers from the River or Assaba regions, Imraguen fishermen from the north, Nemadi hunters from the east... there were lots of foreigners, especially Senegalese, but also Moroccans, Algerians, Tunisians and Malians. All kept to themselves because the city had rejected them. The people who'd been born in the place had no past and no pride. They all dreamed of emigrating to the megacities of the Gulf, or to even more distant rich places.

I wanted to find a hotel or rent an apartment, but Aziza said, 'No way, we're going to my sister's!'

Aziza's sister lived in an enormous house in a peaceful, wealthy district. Uniformed men were stationed outside large gates to watch over the light sleep of the powerful. We had to announce ourselves at one of these gates. Cheibou and I exchanged a glance: this didn't look like much fun.

It was Gallia who came to open the door for us. The two sisters squealed with joy and kissed each other repeatedly. Gallia was an even skinnier version of Aziza. Her complexion was milkier than her sister's, her lips thinner, and her eyes lacked the mischievous sparkle of my friend's.

Gallia's husband was waiting for us in the plush living room. He was a tall, thin man, dressed in a suit that was a little tight on him and a sober tie. He had eyes that drilled into you. 'Mamine is a judge,' his wife told us. I saw Cheibou stiffen and stand up straighter, the playfulness in his eyes fade. He whispered some words to Aziza that I couldn't hear. Her lips made the shape of 'you dirty faggot'. We were served *mechoui,* spit-roasted lamb. Aziza and her sister chatted, the judge talked on the phone, Cheibou kept staring at the couches, the cushions, the gilt-edged furnishings, the ceiling.

Aziza introduced me as the best friend she'd ever had and Cheibou as practically her little brother. Cheibou winced noticeably at that. When the judge heard the reason for my trip, he asked if I had a photo of my sister. I had one in my bag, which I handed to him. 'You won't have to look for her,' he said, 'I'll give this photo to the police and they'll find her, wherever she is.'

'You're not going to publish it in the press?'

'Why not? It would be a good way of finding her.'

'She'd refuse to see me again and hate me forever.'

'All right, don't worry. It won't appear in the press. Only the police will see it, and I'll tell them to be as discreet as possible.'

'She left,' I added, 'with a man who was older than her, in his thirties perhaps. He was tall, black, he called himself Alain, or Allan, something like that. He said he was French, but he spoke with a strong African accent. She met him in Atar, in a hostel where she was working.'

'They'll find her,' Mamine assured me. 'Especially if she's with a foreigner—since the terrorist attacks, all foreigners are under surveillance! Be patient, and don't try anything on your own, it could spoil things. I'll take care of it.'

I felt euphoric. You see, I told my sister inside my head, I'm not abandoning you. I'll knock on the gates of hell to find you. I'll prize open the jaws of monsters to save you from their sharp teeth. I'll face anything the world throws at me. I'll deny my own joys. I'll trample on sacred books just to hold you in my arms. If you come back to me, I'll celebrate you every day. Maybe I'll even forget this absurd infatuation that's taken hold of me, because my heart will be full of you. I'll even be wise, if you want me to!

After dinner, Cheibou excused himself, saying, 'I must leave you now, I've got friends waiting for me. I'll be back to kiss you soon, my darlings.' Aziza thundered, 'You're abandoning us already, you dirty—!' She glanced around her, then finished, 'Traitor!' But the mistress of the house stood up immediately to see Cheibou to the door, clearly not desperate to hold him back.

I didn't leave the house for the rest of the day. Visions of Louad kept swimming into my consciousness: its sober little houses, slightly higgledy-piggledy; its pure white tents; my aunt walking with confidence despite her blindness; Yacoub and his disarming naivety, the sheikh's mother, so gentle, laughing and kind, with her accent from the far south. And the sheikh. I imagined him free of his chains, his childhood, the absurd title chance had bestowed on him, the beliefs that imprisoned him. He was still so young, yet he was trapped in a maze of archaic dogma. I imagined him as my own, and the life we would choose together: I'd give up everything, close my house, renounce my friendships, my habits, my fickle passions. I'd open my eyes in his arms. I thought I could already feel them. But reality soon returned to chase my illusions away. I made myself focus again on what I was there for: my sister, lost in the midst of this heartless bastard of a city.

I was getting impatient, but Aziza and Gallia reassured me: 'Mamine has sent several policemen after her. They'll find her.'

'But she's not a criminal,' I said, 'I don't want her arrested or questioned. She'd never forgive me.'

'No, no,' they replied, 'all they'll do is locate her. They'll tell Mamine where she is and then you can go and meet her.'

Cheibou came over in the mornings, when the judge wasn't home. He'd make tea for us, spar with Aziza, then leave again quickly. He explained that he'd met some musicians who were teaching him to play the guitar.

Sam called every day. He said he was bored without us, and passed on the news: my cousin Yacoub was still in police hands, but he'd seen him and he was doing OK. The administration seemed unwilling to listen to the sheikh, who remained determined to reject the dam. Zeinab had a new lover. A few drops of rain had fallen and he'd almost finished his book of poetry. I was furious that Yacoub was still in prison and that I could do nothing to help him. But I was far away, powerless, and my sister might be waiting for me in some corner of this huge, indifferent city.

In the evenings, Gallia would take us out to dinner in what she called 'fashionable' restaurants. We'd watch people prostrating themselves before the god of money, parading their wealth: suits from the best boutiques, jewellery that weighed on their necks and wrists, silk veils perfectly paired with expensive shoes and bags, intricately embroidered *boubous*. They talked but never laughed too loudly, and they looked at the waiters with a gaze I interpreted as studied contempt. Nothing about them rang true. Aziza and I watched them and said nothing. We'd already had enough of this shining superfluity: we missed the wild festivity of our lives and our friends in Atar, where we lived without watching each other doing it. Of course we liked to have fun, of course we took our lovers' money, but we were not fixated on appearances. This pompous vulgarity was alien and sickening to us.

One evening, Cheibou invited us to one of his friends' parties. Aziza dragged her hesitant sister along; it was an evening of *bendja*, an old slaves' dance that we knew from Atar and that I'd always adored, with its risqué words and frantic contortions. There wasn't much of an audience, mainly a lot of gays gesticulating furiously while they talked, and some young women who were too well-dressed for us. Gallia wanted to go home. 'I can't stay here,' she said, 'my husband...' Aziza held her back. 'Your husband won't know anything about it, and besides, we're your guests, so if you don't stay with us, we won't come back to your place.' Gallia sat back down, but placed her veil over her face.

A woman, in her fifties, still very beautiful, walked slowly into the middle of the crowd. She started dancing, at first just with her fingertips, looking to the left and then to the right in a rhythmic movement. The tam-tam and the *tidinitt* accompanied her gestures. She began to sway slowly, then to sing in a powerful voice:

> *Look at me, look at me closely.*
> She swayed her body.
> *So why did he leave me?*
> She held out her arms.
> *See how smooth they are, the arms on which he rested.*
> *So why did he leave me?*

She caressed her breasts:

> *See the beautiful melons I have here, that he loved to smell.*
> *So why did he leave me?*

She touched her belly:

> *See my smooth belly and what I hide below it, that he loved to honour.*
> *So why did he leave me?*

She uncovered her plump legs:

> *Look at my legs, what could be more beautiful?*
> *He loved to caress them.*
> *So why did he leave me?*

She turned and shook her round buttocks.

> *See for yourself this behind that drove him to a frenzy.*
> *Why did he leave me?*
> *Someone's put a curse on him, my man!*

Then she whirled around as if possessed by *jinns*.

Aziza jumped into the circle and started to accompany the dancer. I did the same. Cheibou swung us both around. We left very pleased with our evening. Even Gallia had to admit she'd had a good time.

The judge was waiting for us at home. He had some news. My sister had split up with the foreigner, who'd then left the country, and struck up a relationship with a young man called Khaled. The two of them had been arrested for drug possession and spent a few days in jail. They'd disappeared from circulation for a while after that, before setting sail illegally for the Canary Islands. There'd been no sign of them since. I broke down in tears. I asked God what I'd done to deserve the people I loved always running away from me. Why did misfortune keep pursuing me? I swore to my sister inside my head that I'd never have forced her into anything, would never have refused her anything. All I ever wanted was to love her.

I didn't sleep a wink that night. I tossed and turned in the bedroom, while Aziza and her sister took turns sitting with me. 'I'm fine, go to sleep, I'm fine,' I told them, 'I just don't feel like sleeping tonight.' They ignored my protests and spent the night stroking my hands and comforting me.

The next day I was surprised to feel a little better, but I still couldn't relax. I was impatient to escape the capital, with its false promises that had ensnared my sister and continued to torment other people every day. Why this attraction for the new? Did no one realise happiness was not to be found in a place, that it lived in our hearts, that it could be invented, and false, and could bend in the slightest wind? What were these reckless young people looking for when they fled to the cities of the rich world: rejection? Racism? The slum quarters of ugly towns? Had no one told them luxury was not available to the wretched? As for this Khaled character, who'd dragged my sister into all of that; I wanted to eat his liver, and his guts, and his heart. I wanted to tear him apart with my fingers, to castrate him, to impale him...

I woke Aziza.

'My friend, I have to leave. You stay with your sister for a few more days.'

'Are you crazy?' she said, 'You want me to die of boredom? I'm coming home with you, to our house, to my house.'

I called Cheibou, who said he'd come right away. The judge and his wife were already on their feet. I thanked them profusely. They pressed us to stay with them a few days longer. I apologised and declined. Outside, Cheibou was already waiting in front of my car. He said, 'Actually, I've just come to say hello. I'm not coming back with you. I'm going to carry on learning the guitar.'

'I understand,' I said, 'I'll miss you, my friend.' I kissed him.

Aziza shouted, 'So, you're letting us down, you scumbag? You've been waiting for this, to come here and let us down, eh, you little bastard?' She hugged him then, saying, 'It's all right, I love you, you dirty faggot!' Cheibou burst into tears. 'And I love you, you naughty bitch!'

We set off. I couldn't wait a minute longer. Something, I don't know what, was calling me back to Louad.

But it was Louad that came to me. Sam met me outside my house. 'I've missed you!' he said. 'And guess what? I've just had a call: the sheikh and some of his followers left Louad an hour ago. They're coming here on foot, across the mountain, to see the prefect.'

I decided to go and meet them.

'Get some rest, you must be exhausted. I'll go,' said Sam.

'No,' I insisted, 'I'll go.'

We watched them descend, patiently, painfully. Most of them supported themselves on sticks. We spotted the sheikh making his way nimbly down the rocks, then reaching out a hand to his friends to help them. They kissed his hands, he exchanged some words with them, then he headed towards us.

'Here we are in your good city of Atar,' he said. 'I'm happy to see you both again.'

I didn't bother with the formalities. I said, 'Yacoub is still in their jail. They may have tortured him.'

The briefest shadow passed across the sheikh's face. He didn't seem to be listening. 'You'll both come with us,' he said, 'if you don't mind. The prefect is expecting us. I hope this question of the dam will be resolved today.'

I offered him my car, but he declined. 'We'll all go together, on foot.'

As we walked, almost every person we passed came over to greet the sheikh and kiss his hand. Some of them followed us, and soon we formed a long procession. We crossed the town trailing a cloud of dust and a lot of noise behind us. Religious litanies were sung and the sheikh kept stopping to kiss children and touch men's heads. By the time we'd got to the prefecture, we were a large crowd. Guards blocked our path. An officer came out and shouted, 'The prefect will receive the sheikh and only a few of his entourage. Everyone else must disperse!' The sheikh called two of his companions, and to my astonishment, me. 'You're a daughter of Louad,' he said.

We went in. It was strange to see the sheikh bow low to the prefect, smiling, holding his hand over his heart, full of deference. The prefect seemed more than anything to be surprised at my presence: he stared at me intently. I thought he was about to address me, but he turned to the sheikh.

'When I received your request for an audience, I immediately accepted it.'

'May God preserve you, Prefect. My name is Qotb. I am your humble servant and the modest sheikh of a brotherhood of poor souls dedicated to God.'

'I know you, Sheikh, and your brotherhood, which has always been peaceful and has always respected the wishes and orders of the administration.'

'Respecting power is a key credo of our order.'

'That's precisely why I'm now truly astonished by the stance you're taking.'

'Perhaps that's because we haven't met before. God's creatures need to talk to each other in order to hear each other.'

'I sent an emissary, and the mayor came in person.'

'Their speeches seem to have drowned in a flood of words. You know, Prefect, words can sometimes be distorted by arrogance…'

'The mayor came back outraged by your attitude. One of your followers insulted him.'

'Insulting people is prohibited by our path. I'm ready to ask forgiveness and to kiss the mayor's feet if he felt, for a single minute, insulted by one of ours.'

'The mayor was the bearer of a message.'

'Forgive me, Prefect, but I'm afraid the mayor himself didn't fully understand the message.'

'What do you mean?'

'He offered us nothing but the abandonment of our path.'

'We're not concerned with your path. This is simply about the building of the dam.'

'We understand, Prefect, your desire to build this nation, but this dam cannot be built over people's dead bodies.'

'You mean…?'

'I mean, Prefect, that for those of us who follow this path, Louad is our destiny. It's our promised land, it's where the exile of our Great Sheikh ended. We cannot abandon it without dying ourselves.'

'Who's asking you to abandon it?'

'The dam, Prefect…'

'What about it?'

'A dam could be a gift from God, I understand, because it brings water, life, work. But Louad was not chosen for the riches of this world. It was chosen to be the cave that shelters our prayers for the whole world.'

'Louad is an oasis that belongs to a country. It's subject to the law, just like anywhere else.'

'You know very well that we obey the law and respect the authorities. But we're afraid, Prefect.'

'Of what?'

'Of having to disobey you. Of seeing a dam erected that we reject.'

'Why would you reject it?'

'Because there are laws that pre-existed our country and our world, laws that God gave us and that today's laws must respect. Our primary law is that we must worship the creator.'

'I don't want to get into these considerations. My first concern is respect for the law.'

'And the general interest?'

'And the general interest!'

'And development? I mean, what is now called development?'

'Yes, development! I know your path is not in favour of progress.'

'It's not opposed to it in principle, and it's even prepared to contribute to it. Prefect, I'm going to offer you a proposal that addresses your concerns and ours. It will, if you accept it, be a sign of our loyalty to the state.'

'I'm listening.'

'I propose, if you agree, Prefect, to finance, from our order's own resources, the research for a dam, in every way similar to the one you want to build here, in any other oasis you designate. That way the state won't have wasted its money in vain, and the region will still benefit from a new dam.'

'Can you afford that?'

'We make sure to provide ourselves with the means to achieve our ambitions. We will do everything we can. We have a lot of loyal followers and a lot of friends.'

'Your proposal may be of interest to us, but I can't give you an answer without consulting my superiors. I must warn you however, that any breaches of order will not be tolerated.'

'We've never called for disorder, Prefect. We've always respected the administration.'

'Your cousin Mohand came to see me. He's in favour of the dam.'

'My cousin Mohand left Louad a long time ago. He has his own ideas now.'

'Ideas that are perhaps shared by some of your followers.'

'I'm not aware at present of any dissenting voices in our ranks. I'd gladly listen to any opinion that came to light. I am only the sheikh and the voice of our brotherhood.'

'You're a remarkable sect.'

'We're not a sect, Prefect. We're an order, and we open our arms to the whole world.'

'All the same, you're very strange.'

'Perhaps, Prefect, but we do no harm to anyone. We don't

reject or despise anyone and we abhor violence. Our path is founded on love, admittedly immoderate, of the creator and of creation.'

'This conversation is over. I've taken note of your proposal, and as a sign of my goodwill towards you, I'll immediately order the release of your young follower, Yacoub.'

'Thank you, Prefect, for listening to me. As for the release of our son Yacoub, please note that I did not request it.'

'Why not? Isn't he one of yours?'

'He's one of our most promising sons and I have a great deal of love for him. For our path though, there's no prison for anyone who can invoke the creator, even if only in spirit. Yacoub's imprisonment is your burden, and that of the mayor, not ours. We will never request the freedom of one of our faithful, even if he's been unjustly arrested. That would be to doubt his faith.'

'He insulted the mayor. But I repeat, I will release him in spite of everything. You can go now, Sheikh.'

The sheikh left, bowing low. I was astonished by his attitude, the way he held himself, full of humility, and the firmness of his words. I followed him to wait for Yacoub outside the police station. The crowd tried to join us but the police turned them back. Sam was already there. He'd brought my car, some clothes for Yacoub, drinks and sandwiches. When Yacoub appeared, he went first to the sheikh to kiss his hand. The sheikh kissed him on the head and said nothing. All the same, I thought I saw a gleam in his eyes.

The sheikh then headed for the mountain, followed by a crowd that had swelled again. Sam tried to dissuade him from a climb that could be difficult, even dangerous.

'This is the only route taken by the followers of renunciation. It's imperative that I follow their example.'

'But you didn't choose renunciation yourself,' said Sam.

'I know, the sheikh of the path should live the life of the common people, because he's the guardian of the common people. But he's also, in a sense, a student of renunciation.'

Sam asked the sheikh about the proposal he'd made to the prefect. He replied, 'Our aim is to preserve Louad from the contamination of modern life, and also to extend a fraternal hand to all those who distrust our path. We're simply seeking the light.'

'But can you really afford to finance this study? Do you know how much it will cost?'

'We considered this proposition carefully. We consulted many of our loyal followers, here at home and even abroad: engineers, financiers, specialists of all kinds. We contacted those of our faithful who could contribute to financing the project. We can get the money we need within a reasonable time. It will cost a lot, but nothing is worth more to us than saving the Medina of our hearts.'

As I watched the sheikh set off, the other faithful following behind him, to conquer that mountain of ours that everyone said was haunted, I felt a stab of loss. It was accompanied by the feeling that I was missing some essential part of me; all that was left of me, perhaps. I couldn't take my eyes off the figure of the sheikh as he moved away, escaping from me, perhaps. I was tempted to run after it, though my legs felt wobbly and my mind foggy. Sam held me back: he thought I was about to fall. But Louad was calling me.

THE SHEIKH

The moment demanded that we make a definitive choice. We no longer had the luxury of long hours of deliberation. The emissary from the prefect came. He didn't speak this time, just handed me his message and left. It said the authorities could not accept my proposal, the dam would be built as soon as possible, and the first teams would be arriving soon. I also learned that my friend José had been dismissed.

I didn't know why the world was being so hard on us, a small oasis populated by gentle people who'd never harmed anyone; who wanted only to pray and live humbly in faith. But the state should have understood that by planning the dam, it was planning our destruction, the end of our aspirations, perhaps even the extinction of our path. I, the shepherd of that path, no longer knew what direction to take. I couldn't accept our death, but I was afraid of violence and hatred. I was afraid of what would happen if we refused, but we had to refuse.

Saara's return had disturbed me too. She came back to Louad ill, dizzy and unable to stand, shaking with fever. She stayed with my mother because her blind cousin couldn't look after her. José examined her, said it was just exhaustion and would pass, but she looked so shaky when I saw her. So beautiful, too. In her weary eyes, I thought I read a plea. Another one I couldn't answer. Her friend, the deaf-mute, arrived to help care for her. I called Sam the poet too. One day, I thought, he could speak the truth about our situation. But which truth?

To try to find out, to decipher the ideas that echoed around my head, I climbed the mountain alone one night to visit the followers of renunciation. They squeezed a little tighter into their hut to make room for me. I knelt down next to my father's old friend Memine, the Master of the path. I whispered into the dark.

'I've tried everything, Master. They've rejected everything. They want the dam. I can't accept that, but I don't know how to refuse it. I have no real answer to the fury that's coming towards us. It's dark, Master. The son of the Great Sheikh can't see a thing.'

'The son of the Great Sheikh should not be looking with his eyes.'

'I've meditated, Master. I've thought a lot. I can't see anything. I don't know how to interpret the signs of this new world.'

'Perhaps that's because you're trying to understand them.

Don't try to read them. They're just fleeting appearances that deceive.'

'Is the dam they want to build just an appearance, Master? Or their stubborn determination to destroy us? Or Mohand, who's trying to have me banished? Or their hatred for our path? Or José, our doctor and friend, who they expelled?'

'Those are all just tricks of time, vulgar illusions. Our faith is in ourselves. The rest is nothing.'

'But I have to manage that time. I have to preserve a land for our followers and for our path. I have to preserve my father's legacy.'

'All of that is meaningless.'

'Preserving the path is not meaningless!'

'Only the precepts of the path matter.'

'I know, the precepts. And you, up here, are the fulfilment of them.'

'We dream of fulfilling them.'

'I know, Master, I'm the leader of the world of appearances, you are the guardians of the secret.'

'Which we're only trying to reach, through faith.'

'You are the pinnacle.'

'Climbers ascending towards the pinnacle.'

'Master, I'm getting everything mixed up... I want to preserve Louad and I no longer know how. The forces of evil want to uproot us from our soil.'

'What do you intend to do, Sheikh?'

'I spoke their language, but they refused to listen.'

'Will they hear you again?'

'I don't think so, and when I called for you, you didn't say a word!'

'We don't use the language of words.'

'But I need you!'

'We're from another place.'

'And I'm the keeper of the valley, the *barzakh* that separates one world from another, the bare ground that leads to the true path, yours, that of annihilation in God. I'm the manager of the world of appearances, of simple faiths that can only fumble towards clarity. But the world of appearances is now in need of the enlightened ones!'

'Such pretension, my son! We are by no means enlightened. We only take the path of self-annihilation that leads towards the light.'

'I'm alone, Master. I'm lost. I don't know what to do.'

'You're the one we've chosen to walk the earth. It's true that you carry the *baraka* of your father, but we chose you above all because we sensed in you both an attraction to the sublime and a practical intelligence. We took care of your education, we instilled in you the strength to lead, and we surrounded you with a *jemaa* of experts in the sciences of the external world. All of this was so that we could gather here in peace. Your role is to manage the first stages of the path, and to preserve Louad as a shelter for our followers. Here we are at the next stage, that of rupture and fasting.'

'Today, Master, I need to hear what you have to say.'

'We no longer know how to speak. You will return to your world and you will pray, and listen again to the breath inside you. That's all.'

'The breath hasn't spoken to me.'

'It will speak if you listen.'

'Master... I would like to stay here a little longer.'

'You must go back down, my son, to your people.'

'But Master…'

'I know, my son. You're alone. Perhaps you're unhappy. That is your destiny. Don't come here again, unless it is to pray or to die.'

The whole of Louad was there, gathered after the evening prayer. Old men with weary faces, wrapped up in thick *burnous*, adults hugging their waists in loose *boubous* that billowed in the evening breeze, teenagers in everyday clothes, with questions in their eyes. The women showed only their faces or their hands. Some of the followers of renunciation were there too, their heads bowed so they didn't see too much of the hustle and bustle of life.

They were all there because I'd summoned them. I wanted them to understand the dangers that lay ahead, and to give their opinions, before I, in the name of our path, expressed any opinion or laid down any rule that would become definitive.

That evening, I'd forbidden any ethereal elevation, any collective or individual ecstasy and even any session of *dhikr* that was too noisy. I wanted the people to have their minds firmly on earthly things to make their judgement: the order was about to experience changes that would resonate for a very long time, perhaps forever.

Mehmed spoke first, on my behalf.

'Brothers and sisters in God, the sheikh wants you to know that he is aware that this is an unusual gathering. Our wise men, the companions of our guide and the father of us all, the Great Sheikh, are here with us. They could have deliberated alone and given voice to their knowledge. But the sheikh felt that today we are all faced with choices that must necessarily lead us towards new destinies. As you know, the authorities asked repeatedly for a school to be opened in Louad. The sheikh agreed to that request, despite the excellent intellectual and spiritual nourishment we already provide for our children. However, the administration has drawn up a second project, this time for the construction of a dam in our oasis.

You all know that this land was chosen by our Great Sheikh, may Allah be gratified, as a place of prayer, a refuge for our worship, the Medina of our path. We didn't come here for riches or vanity. We came to worship God, for we know he created the *jinn* and mankind only to worship him. We've come here to escape the rest of the world and follow our path in peace, a path we do not force anyone else to follow, but which we would like to see respected. The Great Sheikh dedicated this land to work and faith alone.

The problem is that this dam will lead to a new form of cultivation that will destroy the land. It will lead to the arrival of hundreds, even thousands of people who will neither embrace nor respect our path. It will turn us into pariahs in the oasis that we created. In this land of worship, it will install the pursuit of gain. This dam will drive us away from Louad. The Great Sheikh, our guide to the truth and the father of us all, said, 'Louad is the oasis where our quest ends, our path has no salvation but here, this is the Medina of our path. Are we going to let the Medina of our path be destroyed?'

I signalled to Mehmed to cut short his emotive speech. He'd gone further than I meant him to. I'd just wanted him to spell out the situation in plain language. I was looking for the answer to a single question: what should we do?

The floor was given over to the ten friends of the Great Sheikh. They said that Satan, the enemy of all human faiths, had appeared in Louad and wanted to destroy the work of our order. They said that Louad was God's land, a pure place where he could be worshipped without pause, that this land was holy and must be protected from the rottenness that was now assailing hearts and disturbing minds.

They said our path knew of no other *hijrah*, and that Louad, as Mehmed had said, was indeed the Medina of all those who embraced the teachings of the Great Sheikh. For them therefore, there was no question of building a dam that would necessarily take Louad away from those who knew no other empire than that of the path. They did however, insist on what they repeated were core tenets of the path: respect for earthly powers and the rejection of all violence.

The crowd mumbled silent prayers and uttered the occasional approving '*Wallahi*'. But there was an uproar when Mohand stood up. With a gesture, I demanded silence and invited him to speak.

'Dear brothers,' he said, 'some people are protesting my presence here and railing against me. Should I remind them that I am a son of Louad and of the path, that my forefathers were *ulama*, that I am the nephew of the Great Sheikh and that in any case, whispers and evil words should have no place in our path?

We talk of Louad being in imminent danger. Where is that danger? I'd like to see the murderous hydra that's lying in wait for us and against which, alongside all of you, I'd engage in the fiercest of battles. But I see nothing, and yet I swear to you I'm not blind and I have no need of a guide.

They say the state is planning to build a dam here. Why should Louad complain, that amongst a thousand possible oases, it's the one that's been chosen to house such a useful structure? Do you know what a dam is? It's water, in abundance, that resource that's so lacking in our regions, such a precious commodity here, blessed by God. Why would anyone in their right mind oppose water? We're told that our brotherhood would risk obliteration if it accepted the dam. This is not so. In a thousand other places, Sufi brotherhoods have built dams and continued to thrive. Why should our brotherhood reject this dam? Because it would have to share Louad with other communities? Why should this offend us?

We're also told that the Great Sheikh declared that Louad could only belong to the path. He didn't write that in any of his books! Some of his companions, present here today, have claimed to have heard him say this. Why should we believe them?

Don't let yourselves be led by old dogmas that have become obsolete, by a sheikh who's influenced by his mother, a foreign slave, and by a *jemaa* made up of senile old men. Look around you and wake up: the world has changed!'

A clamour erupted. I heard insults and saw clenched fists. I appealed to the faithful for calm, but inside I was perplexed and furious. Why had Mohand suddenly decided to confront me and to publicly insult the ten friends of the Great Sheikh? He could have asserted his convictions without hurting anyone. Where had that hateful look on his face come from, and even the courage to challenge us directly, he who I knew to be a coward? I realised that this was a new test for our order. Mohand was trying to open up a breach in our ranks. Behind him, almost certainly, was the administration.

Shouts were still coming from the crowd, and I still wanted to hear Mohand explain his thinking. I stood up, and contrary to our custom, spoke.

'My fathers, mothers, brothers and sisters, the sheikh is usually the last to speak, but I can't allow foul words to ring out in a circle of followers of the path. Please listen in silence and wait your turn to speak! Mohand, my cousin, you may continue.'

'I've finished, cousin,' he replied. A sound of thunder went up from the crowd. Some people shook their fists at him. He hadn't called me 'Sheikh'. I wondered to myself how long he'd been ranting inwardly against the path and against me. I prayed silently to God to spare me the undignified anger and secret hatred that could eat away at hearts. I spoke again.

'My dear brothers, I forbid anyone to say an unpleasant word or touch a hair on my cousin's head. He has spoken in terms that do not please us. But does he have to say things that make us happy? He presented his truth. I demand that we respect it and respond to him without forgetting the precepts of our path.'

Young Yacoub stood up. I almost forbade him to speak, for I could see the anger in him and feared that the ardour of youth would carry him too far. But the crowd was already cheering him on.

'My gracious Sheikh, my fathers, mothers, brothers and sisters, this man you see here, this traitor who dares to speak of our sheikh and our elders in these terms, is unworthy to be among us. This man has not stopped at that. Since his return, the extent of his hatred of our order has come to light. He pushed the authorities to go ahead with the dam project. He even asked them to banish the sheikh. You heard! This man must leave our assembly immediately. Otherwise, my gracious Sheikh, I will answer for nothing!'

There were shouts. I saw men preparing to attack Mohand. I had to intervene again so that he could retreat in peace.

'My brothers and sisters,' I said, 'my fathers and mothers, come to your senses! Don't let yourselves be carried away by rage, the offspring of Satan. We have an essential matter to decide, so let's think clearly, rid ourselves of anger. Let us forget treachery and decide in peace!'

I still felt troubled. I saw that events would soon be out of my hands, out of all of our hands; that we were chasing to catch up with time and could not hesitate any longer.

Yacoub addressed the crowd again, and his words frightened me. 'I know the world that this villain Mohand was talking about. It's a world that believes only in market values, that is gradually eating away at certainties and faiths. It's a world that knows only one law, the law that our path has always rejected, the law of the strongest! I ask our elders and our sheikh to reflect on this. We cannot blindly reject the use of all possible weapons when not only our path, but also our faith, are in danger of disappearing, of being obliterated by the ugly powers of this age!'

I couldn't suppress a shudder when approving cries rang out in answer to Yacoub's words.

I could no longer think. A knot of anguish strangled my throat. I raised my hand, and without really considering it, called for the prayer of fear. A tremor ran through my body, and through the whole audience. The prayer of fear had never been called on by our order. None of my fathers had ever done it, even at the worst of times, but on that day I saw the terrible need. I could sense something crumbling around me, terrible satanic shapes moving across the hitherto calm sky over Louad, the sound of thunder in the distance, and us so weak, preparing to face a hurricane.

The men divided into two groups and took turns praying behind me. They'd never prayed like this before, but they knew the rites. The prayer of fear was an act of war, the only one we allowed ourselves. Some of the faithful were confused by my choice, and tried to make sense of it. Others, like Yacoub, thought they understood it and rejoiced. I heard some people crying. I led the prayer without losing my voice, then turned towards the faithful, lowered my head, closed my eyes and retreated inside myself.

There was a terrifying silence. The void was calling out to me. White dunes were offering themselves to my spirit, the desert wind was panting inside me. I groped in the darkness of our burning Saharan sun. How, I asked God, could such light and shadow co-exist? I held my head in my hands and plunged even deeper into the abyss of my being. I told myself this was where reality lay. The feeling was like nausea. I tried to erase all awareness of earthly things, but the first thing to appear in my mind's eye was Saara. She was waiting for me, smiling, on the edge of a precipice. I wrenched myself away from the invitation in her eyes, but I was pulled back, again and again. Finally, I managed to escape her, to sink into soft folds of nothingness, to spin in a space of silence, to press myself into a place of containment, to meet the moment where meaning melts. A light of a different hue began to illuminate my mind. I plunged towards it, still hearing in spite of myself, the voices of Saara and of my friends and companions in thirst, the desert nomads.

It was brief, but it was enough: I'd felt the breath in me. I got straight to my feet to translate it. The assembled people stood up with me. They joined hands.

I said, 'The time has come for our faith to penetrate the deserts, to plumb the depths of the dry wells and to quench its thirst with the only powers our path has given us. The satanic powers whose arrival my father predicted have now reached Louad. They're preparing to crush us, to extinguish the light that has chosen to shine here. What can we do against the Satans of today, who dress themselves in the clothes of the new, of progress, of work, of full bellies? You all know very well, and I will continue to insist on this point, that we're forbidden from raising swords or spears, even from using verbal insults. But you also know that Louad belongs to the path, is our last refuge and the Medina of our Great Sheikh, our beloved father. I declare now, before all of you, that our path rejects the dam, and I swear that I will do everything to prevent the erection of this edifice of lies that will divorce Louad from faith. Together we will refuse every stone. We will lie down before their engines of death, if need be, because Louad belongs to us. The battle we wage will be a battle of certainty. It will not be the outburst of hatred and destruction envisaged by the vulgar enemies of our path.

I repeat once again: neither the friends of the Great Sheikh nor I will accept any violence, or any personal offence against the men who will come here. We must simply smile and refuse. We must remain clean and not allow ourselves to be infected with the impurities of these times. May God protect our path.'

Just as I finished speaking, Saara's friend Jid, the deaf-mute beggar, stood up in the middle of the crowd and shouted, 'The men who are threatening you destroyed me! Don't let them destroy you too!'

Cries went up and people gathered around the beggar. Both men and women were in tears. 'The deaf-mute has spoken!' they cried, 'He can hear! It's a miracle!' Some said, 'It's a prophesy of our victory!' I didn't know what to think. Jid was praised, lifted above the crowd, everyone reaching out to touch him and share his grace.

The faithful came forward in turn to kiss my hands. I blessed them, and prayed softly to God that these men and women would not be swept away by the ill winds, crushed by the blind cogs of the machinery of modernity.

THE BEGGAR

I was living in a nightmare. My whole existence, I felt, could only be a dream sent to torment me. It couldn't be my here and now. My eyes felt open, but perhaps they were really closed; perhaps I was tossing and turning in a restless sleep, and one day I'd wake up. It didn't seem possible that I was seeing what I was seeing: my mother still suffering, my heart pierced by her pleas, my forehead tight with pain, the stench of our hut, the air outside it, the indifferent sun, the burning rocks that I still had to cross every day to go for alms. Even Saara, who was gone, and the sheikh, and Louad, trampled underfoot, razed to the ground by barbarian hordes, and all the people down there in the town, still loving, still gorging themselves on food. There was something wrong with it all. It couldn't be real.

I felt utterly alone. Everything was silent or moaning in pain. I couldn't summon the will to go to town and beg. Saara's friends had left, the place was dead. Sam had hidden himself away somewhere in the rubble of poetry and inebriation. Moustaff the Horrible was exulting.

When I came back to my mother, I was aching all over. I was covered in bruises and my flesh and heart were bleeding. I found my mother writhing, vicious claws of pain ripping through her body. Her face was bare. When I addressed her, she opened her eyes and raised her head. Joy at seeing me again lit up her features for a second, before the pain claimed her again. Mama sat beside her, sobbing: she had no idea what to do.

I went outside to try to steady my breathing and compose my thoughts. The mountain was sleeping, oblivious to my suffering. No voices reached me from Louad. In the distance, the lights of the city were flickering on.

I stayed there, prostrate at the threshold of our hut, for a long time, my own thoughts and emotions lost to me, inhabited by emptiness, anaesthetised against the moment, insensitive to the sorrows that pressed against my body, clamouring to enter. Suddenly something jolted me, and I began to move, like a sleepwalker, towards the only chink of light that offered itself, the only exit from my tunnel of despair.

For too long I'd hesitated, daydreamed, dozed. It was time to leave my cave, to forget the spasms of hunger, the deceptive hopes and the fear of extinction that haunted me. I'd been carrying my misery and anguish around with me for too long. For too long I'd lived in exile from everything, allowing not an ounce of pleasure for my mother or myself. For too long I'd been replaying that ancient scene: my body whipped, my insides soiled, my humanity crushed; the jeers of those pigs as they lashed out at me, laughing while I struggled and screamed, hitting me in the face to make me shut up. I didn't shut up, but no one came to help me, because those pigs were the gilded youth of the town, the apples of their foul, corrupt parents' eyes, the *crème de la crème* of evil, adored by all, and I was a voiceless parasite.

In Louad, too, they'd taken everything. They'd destroyed the people and the spirit of the place. Saara and the sheikh were gone, defeated, broken. I didn't think I'd ever see them again.

But now I knew the path I had to take: not to heal my wounds, but to numb them. To take back something for myself, to prevent me from dying inside, to finally silence the vile voice that whispered from inside me, 'You're not a man, you're a stinking turd. All you can do is reach your hand out for coins. You can't call yourself human: you live nowhere, you own nothing, you wear rags, you can't look after your mother, you couldn't do anything for Saara. All you have is the stench you carry in your arse, in your very entrails, the pestilence of their presence in your body that you live with every day, that assaults you in your dreams and denies you all joy. When will you do something to save what can still be saved in you?'

The evidence paraded itself before me: the obvious, raging truth, the lightning strike that was needed to defeat them, to make them scream, to put fear on their ugly faces and to worm its way into their souls, never to leave, waking them up at night, allowing them no peace. I knew where to go. I'd located the thunder that would shake them to their corrupt cores. I would find my pride again, avenge my mother, avenge Saara.

SAARA

Salem was the caretaker of the mayor's large palm grove. I knew him well. Early in the mornings, when I crossed the *battha*, the sandy border that separated the oasis from the town, I'd see him sitting in front of his hut, preparing tea. Sometimes he'd call me over and offer me some bread, and I'd sit there waiting for the little glass of tea he'd serve me. Sometimes he sent me into town to fetch sugar or food for him. I ran quickly and he gave me a coin or two when I got back. Salem was a good man, but I knew what he sold in secret: huge sprays of fire that shattered rocks to dig wells and draw water up from the depths. Sam described them whenever he came back from the oases. He said they ripped open the earth and stole what it had hidden away: waters not meant for now, but reserved for other times, other peoples, decades, centuries perhaps, in the future, snatched away by the machines of death to be offered to the impatient rich of today. Future generations, Sam said, would be left with dead land that could never be revived because its depths were permanently dry. They would cry theft, treason… poor peasants were already seeing their crops and palm trees die, because the big landowners were using pumps of all kinds, solar and non-solar, to draw up the ground water for themselves. Sam said that rocky ground didn't stop them: they used dynamite to blast away the stones, uncovering water that only they could reach. They watered their palms generously, gave their animals something to drink, treated themselves to swimming pools under the greedy skies, and later they bought the land of their poorer neighbours at a bargain price, when the neighbours were obliged to sell off properties that no longer earned them anything.

I'd often heard huge explosions shake the mountain, over to the west, where they were digging up the road. There'd be a terrifying roar followed by a landslide that shook the earth. I sometimes thought our little hut was going to fly away, that we'd be buried beneath piles of rubble. I understood then that mountains could also be violated, that no matter how many millennia had passed since they first raised their heads, they were powerless to prevent immense passages being blasted through their bodies.

Salem hid this stone-shaking thunder in his palm grove; he didn't tell anyone except his customers where it was, but I knew, because I was deaf and people talked in front of me. I'd heard him explain in detail what needed to be done to let these cruel machines express themselves. There were small parts, called detonators, and other parts like candles. All you had to do was stick the detonator into the spark plugs, attach wires to it and light it. Salem had explained this to one of his buyers in front of me. He added that it was very dangerous, that you had to get away from the explosion quickly. He also insisted that it be kept secret. The sale was illegal because only the authorities had the right to possess this stuff: owning it legally required a lot of paperwork and it took months to get the necessary authorisations. That was why he was selling these things at such a high price. In fact, it was the mayor who owned these machines of death. Salem sold them for him. The mayor owned everything in the town: the cars, the houses, the offices, the Central Market, now Louad. Even death; he owned that too.

I knew where Salem stashed all the separate components of the explosives, each in its own little safe, in the four corners of the palm grove.

It was dark, but this time the night didn't frighten me. I ran down the mountain without looking around me. The cool sand of the *battha* scratched my bare feet, used to stones. It worked its way into my tiny cuts, causing me some pain and delaying me a little. But I had time on my side: Salem would already be asleep, the palm grove was huge, and no one would hear my footsteps.

Opening the safes was easy. I'd brought a small iron bar with me. All I had to do was twist it in the padlocks. It made very little noise. I performed the operation three times and ended up with a pile of paraphernalia that terrified me at first: this equipment seemed diabolical, a sleeping death.

I stood there, stunned, for several minutes, unable to grasp how easily I'd accomplished this break-in, how quickly I'd crossed the threshold. I thought about putting everything back, but then I heard their laughter, saw their ugly, mocking faces again. I felt the pain again, in my whole body and in the depths of my being, and the disgust and hatred returned. I set about assembling the various parts of the machine's body. 'It's nothing, it's easy.' Salem had told his customers. It was true. I quickly managed to position the parts. Then I put everything in a big bag I'd found in the field and set off running.

The city glittered with a thousand lights, the din of the party set the skies ablaze and the mountain echoed the sounds back again. A huge crowd was gathered outside the auditorium. I didn't go too close, but I heard a young man say to his friend, 'Khaled's having a great time, going after all the girls, marrying when he wants, then divorcing, then going after more girls, then marrying again… it's great when you're rich and can do whatever you like!' A shiver ran through me, rage rose in my throat. Khaled was the mayor's only son, the leader of the gang who'd put the pain inside me, robbed me of my trust, of my reasons to love myself. I almost cried. But I told myself I was going to wipe the contentment from their faces with one proud, magical glow, plant in them the fear that had inhabited me for so long. They would never be without worry again, and I'd avenge not only Saara but also the sheikh, Louad and everyone else. They'd be looking behind them at every turn, in case a new rage was coming to crush them. I wasn't sure what to do though: the crowd was rushing at the door to get into the party; the blaring music was bursting my eardrums; my heart was pumping wildly. Then I spotted the shining row of cars belonging to Khaled and his friends, splendid 4x4s with gleaming metal bodies. I squeezed in between them. Nobody shouted at me; everyone was looking the other way. I leaned against the wheel of one of these mastodons, took out my lighter and lit the fuse before moving away, first slowly, then at high speed.

The explosion stopped me in my tracks. I turned round and saw a spray of flames and smoke bursting out from between the cars, heard a tremendous clatter of sheet metal, followed by hysterical screams. People scurried away; some ran straight past me. Pandemonium broke out. The security guards from the Central Market next door came running up, carrying big sticks, looking terrified. I weaved my way between the empty stalls that framed the market and arrived in the courtyard, which was also full of small, closed stalls surrounded by large shops with their shutters down. Suddenly I felt a supreme confidence in myself. I was the vigilante from the films the little beggars always talked about. All I really needed was a horse and a mask. I was now going to dole out justice to the potentate, Moustaff the Horrible, as Saara and Sam called him, the owner of all of this, the puppet master of penury, the director of evil deeds, the destroyer of Louad, the symbol of this city that loathed me, the men and women who didn't see me, for whom I was a mosquito, a snivelling wretch, who was handed a coin out of pity for the deaf-mute sub-human bastard of a deaf-mute mother.

I placed my second device just under the door of a shop, lit it and ran to the other side of the market. This time the explosion was even bigger, instantly igniting all the small shops and wooden stalls, which burst into flames. I went out into the street as the screams started. Men were fleeing in all directions, the crowd leaving the party was still coming, in a huge hubbub. The sound of car horns filled the air. I walked slowly down the main avenue, through all the noise and tumult, the crush of people in panic. No one paid any attention to the little beggar, moving without haste, unconcerned by the chaos.

From the top of the mountain, I contemplated the sight. The huge fire I'd lit licked the sky. I heard muffled rumblings from the market and the sound of the fire brigade's sirens as they arrived; too late as usual. Smoke now enveloped the entire city centre and obscured the adjacent streets. A strange wail emanated from the city. I'd injured it at its core—the showcase for the vulgar pride of the *nouveau riche*—and its Central Market, the trading post for cynicism and souls.

SAARA

I, the poor deaf-mute beggar, son of a deaf-mute beggar, the dregs of humanity, Jid the bastard, had responded to their contempt, to their complacency. 'Burn, Moustaff the Horrible, king of corruption!' I cried to myself, 'Burn, Khaled, son of the Horrible, heir to embezzlement, to theft and the rape of children who've done nothing but be poor and unprotected!' I hadn't burned their bodies, admittedly, I'd only set fire to a small part of their possessions, but was it not enough for a poor beggar to strike at where their consciences were buried, at the filthy money that they adored? Tomorrow, I or others would walk over their bodies, breaking their bones, as they broke my heart and Saara's.

I went to find Saara in Louad. I watched over her all night. I kissed the sheikh's hand and spoke so that people would cry out at the miracle. They surrounded me and I saw that they loved me. I couldn't stay for long, because my mother was waiting for me, but disaster soon struck. They came in the early hours of the morning, just as Louad was waking up. The noise of their engines drowned out the call of the *muezzin*. Their footsteps on the sand sounded like trumpets heralding the end of time. There were many of them, and behind them, huge machines advanced, jaws gaping, ready to swallow up the land and its people.

The sheikh and his followers were already waiting, gathered at the spot where the dam was to be built. They were singing softly of God, their sheikhs and their path. There was not a gesture, not a glance towards the oncoming behemoths. I heard the sheikh say to the soldiers, 'I love you as God's creatures, my brothers. Do your duty, shoot us if that is the mission you've given yourselves. Our own duty is not to abandon this land.' I heard him speak to Yacoub and his friends, who were already surrounding him, their eyes red with anger. He said, 'Get away from me, I don't want protection, because I don't want any form of violence. Our defeat will not be that Louad is taken from us, our defeat will be the day we use any weapon other than the weapon of the spirit. This land is worth dying for, but it's not worth using violence for.'

An officer approached the sheikh. The sheikh listened to him, smiling, respectful. I saw that it was when they were at their most grovelling that they were actually the firmest. The officer went over to his men, hesitated for a moment, came back to the sheikh, spoke to him again, then walked away, agitated. He growled an order. Soldiers wearing masks advanced towards the crowd, which made no movement. Suddenly everyone fell silent, and as they remained motionless, waiting impassively for the attack, young men armed with clubs emerged from who knows where and stood in front of the sheikh. I heard the sheikh shout, 'Cowards, godless men, stand back, I forbid you…' The soldiers threw tear-gas bombs and fired bullets in the air, then rushed towards the inhabitants of Louad. There was confusion, hysteria and screaming. Yacoub and his friends were overpowered and dragged away by the hair. Boots trampled bodies, truncheons fell on heads, men gripped on to soldiers and refused to let go despite the blows that rained down on them. Women protected their children with their bodies. Some men screamed, others already on the ground received blows without complaint. Prayers that sounded like cries of pain rose up to the sky. A huge cloud of dust and laments floated above Louad. I was about to flee the carnage, when I saw Saara. She was running, her hair loose, her fists raised, cursing the soldiers. She made her way through the awful melee. I rushed after her, but I lost her: all I could see around me was pain being dragged away.

They ravaged everything; the people and their pride. They were furious. It was as if this peaceful oasis had stolen something essential from them, and yet the inhabitants had put up no resistance, had covered their heads and wept in silence, accepted the blows, swallowed the insults. The sheikh remained standing, frozen, his eyes closed. Around him, the ten friends of the Great Sheikh chanted prayers. The soldiers did not attack this circle. It was as if something inexpressible forbade them from doing so.

Suddenly, an order was barked and the soldiers withdrew. The fury stopped. A strange silence descended, punctuated with whimpers, gasps and choked sobs. A soldier stepped forward, paper in hand. 'Sheikh Qotb,' he shouted, 'has been ordered to leave the region and not to return until further notice. A car is waiting for him. The rest of you, disperse!' Complaints and cries were heard. The sheikh raised his arm and shouted in a trembling voice, 'Obey now, my brothers. Return to your homes. I will leave. Let no one follow me. I may not come back, but I will always be with you. You must all stay, never leave this land, so that the Medina of our hearts never dies. And never forget the precepts of our faith. I entrust to you my mother, my home and my father's books.' He walked slowly, still uncertain, towards a vehicle indicated by the soldier, parked some distance away. The people of Louad, crying, quietly lamenting, praying softly, watched him go. Suddenly,

Saara emerged from the crowd. She ran up behind the sheikh. He turned round, stopped to wait for her, and they stood there for a moment, face to face. I couldn't hear what they said. After a moment he held out his hand and she took it. He spoke some indistinct words, she nodded, and then they were gone.

I walked towards our hut. For the first time, I noticed it was leaning to one side and was close to collapse. The branches covering it had lost their colour, faded by sun and time. All around us, the inscrutable rocks no longer seemed intent on our protection. I heard the cries of hyenas. They never bothered my mother because she couldn't hear them.

Mama was asleep at the entrance to the hut, moonlight spilling across her face. She was half-clothed and almost beautiful in her sleep. Her young, naked son hugged her belly. I stepped past her quietly and approached my mother. She'd thrown off the dirty sheet that was covering her. She was moaning in her sleep. Spasms were running through her body. She was trembling a little, the pain driving her away from consciousness. 'You've endured so much, Mother,' I told her, 'you've suffered so much that this mountain should be ashamed. Life has given you no respite: you've toiled, you've begged, you've lived for me, I who am nothing, not worth an ounce of your pain. I love you, Mother, I love you to death, I love you as I see you dying. The future has nothing to offer us. Tomorrow doesn't exist for you. It's dark, like your past, like your life. I love you so much, Mother.'

I placed my hand over her mouth and nose. I didn't press hard: her breathing was already weak and ragged. She shuddered. I kept up the pressure. I closed my eyes and saw her go. I felt her body rise and fall, slowly. Finally it rested on the shores of oblivion.

I wandered back outside, turned my face to the sky. A light wind was blowing, but nothing could dry my tears. I gulped and sobbed. I heard, without pleasure now, the din of the city. I saw the flames receding. They'd almost been extinguished, but I knew the fire I'd lit would continue to burn inside me, that the image of my mother's face would always be before me, and so would that of Saara.

GLOSSARY of Arabic, Berber, Wolof, Mandinka and Twi words in the text

Al-Fatiha — the first chapter of the Qur'an, a prayer for guidance and mercy.

Baraka — benediction.

Barzakh — in Islam, a place separating the living from the hereafter or a stage between death and resurrection.

Boubou — a flowing robe.

Burnou — a long, hooded Arab cloak.

Dhikr — a form of Islamic worship, central to Sufism, in which phrases or prayers are repeatedly recited.

Griot — a West African oral historian, storyteller, poet, and/ or musician.

Harmattan — the dry north-easterly trade wind that blows over West Africa from the Sahara.

Hijrah — the journey the Islamic prophet Muhammad and his followers took from Mecca to Medina.

GLOSSARY

Imam — in Sunni Islam, the prayer leader of a mosque.

Jemaa — an assembly.

Jinn — invisible creatures in early pre-Islamic Arabia and later in Islamic culture and beliefs.

Marabout — a Muslim religious leader and teacher who historically had the function of a chaplain serving as part of an Islamic army.

Méchoui — in Maghrebi cuisine, a whole sheep or lamb spit-roasted on a barbecue.

Muezzin — the official who proclaims the call to the prayer five times a day from the mosque.

Qadi — the magistrate or judge of a Muslim shariah court.

Sharif — a nobleman.

Tidinitt — a traditional Mauritanian guitar.

Ulama — Islamic legal scholars.

Wallahi — 'I swear to God'.

Dedalus Africa

Under the editorship of Jethro Soutar and Yovanka Perdigão, Dedalus Africa seeks out high-quality fiction from all of Africa, including parts of Africa hitherto totally ignored by English-language publishers. Titles currently available are:

The Desert and the Drum – Mbarek Ould Beyrouk
Catalogue of a Private Life – Najwa Bin Shatwan
The Word Tree – Teolinda Gersão
The Madwoman of Serrano – Dina Salústio
The Ultimate Tragedy – Abdulai Silá
Our Musseque – José Luandino Vieira
Co-wives, Co-widows – Adrienne Yabouza
Edo's Souls – Stella Gaitano
Tchanaze – Carlos Paradona Rufino Roque
Saara – Mbarek Ould Beyrouk

Forthcoming titles include:

The Fire Within – Touhfat Mouhbare

The Desert and the Drum by Mbarek Ould Beyrouk

Rachael McGill's translation was shortlisted for The Oxford Weidenfeld Translation Prize in 2019. *The Desert and the Drum* won the Ahmadou-Kourouma Prize in 2016.

'*The Desert and the Drum* is a nicely turned novel of the clashes of tradition and modernity – not so much versus each other but the clashes within each. The constricted tribal ways are challenged by modernity but the faults that prove so damaging here are inherent to it: Rayhana is battered and broken by the demands of traditions, the "other world" of modernity is something of a release valve, yet also doesn't offer true escape. Beyond how it treats these themes, much of the appeal of *The Desert and the Drum* is in the presentation of local color, Beyrouk presenting contemporary Mauritania, on its smallest and most isolated scale as well as on the bustling modern-metropolitan one, very nicely through Rayhana and her experiences. So much she experiences is almost beyond words – such as the machinery the foreigners bring for their mining expedition and what they are doing to the land – but that goes just as much for her emotional experiences across her various stations, and her wide-eyed fumbling efforts to express all this that is new and unknown to her (and, often, her tribe) make for an impressive narrative.'

M.A.Orthofer in *The Complete Review*

'…an easy and enjoyable read.' July Blalack in *Arablit*

'...the narrative bristles with interesting characters and essential questions. Also, through Rayhana's gaze, we can see the strangeness of our own contemporary urban lives afresh.'

Marcia Lynx Qualey in *Qantara*

'Translator McGill has found a register that is at once simple and precise, conveying images that spark both surprise and recognition. Take the description of Rayhana's friend regarding her so intently that it seems as if she is trying "to mount the horses of (Rayhana's) words and ride right inside (her)" or this portrayal of her mother, who "had crossed the Sahara of doubt long ago, never to return". Such phrases at once root the story in its setting and convey its sense to readers everywhere. This balancing of the specific and the universal is perhaps the book's greatest strength. Grounded in the traditions that drive it and yet brimming with observations that are true wherever you read them, the novel bears the hallmark of great literature, making one little corner of the world an everywhere in which all manner of people can meet. *The Desert and the Drum* is an exciting and compelling addition to the anglophone library. While it is unreasonable to expect one book to bear the weight of representing an entire nation there is no doubt that this is a great ambassador for Mauritanian literature.'

Ann Morgan in *A Year of Reading the World*

£11.99   ISBN 978 1 910213 79 7   170p   B. Format

Co-wives, Co-wives by Adrienne Yabouza

'At 49, Lidou is in his prime, a prosperous builder of houses in the Central African Republic and the proud husband of two beautiful wives, Ndongo Passy and Grekpoubou. The only cloud on his horizon is the recent onset of impotence, for which he persuades a pharmacist friend to get him some pills. The day after his first dose, Lidou has a heart attack and drops dead, which gives his opportunistic cousin Zouaboua the chance to accuse the two newly-widowed women of poisoning Lidou, so that he can snatch his cousin's property out from under their noses. If they're going to keep what's rightfully theirs, Ndongo Passy and Grekpoubou must fight with all their might against a backdrop of corruption in which bribery oils the wheels of society, eroding decency and loyalty. It's a weighty topic in many ways, but Adrienne Yabouza writes so lightly and colourfully that this is a delight to read.' Alastair Mabbott in *The Herald*

'In a novel suffused with both humour and observations of venality, it is the friendship of the two women who had to share one man that becomes the most notable and unexpected aspect of a novel which, using a straight-forward narrative style, demonstrates the tension between the hold of tradition and the pull of new possibilities.' Declan O'Driscoll in *The Irish Times*

'…the arrival in English of this new voice is worth celebrating.'
Tadzio Koelb in *The Times Literary Supplement*

£9.99 ISBN 978 1 912868 77 3 124p B. Format

The Ultimate Tragedy by Abdulai Silá

'"Mizzes, want houseboy?" is the first line in Abdulai Silá's *The Ultimate Tragedy*. It is an imploration delivered desperately in a flawed Portuguese by Ndani, a poor, illiterate teenage girl, who leaves her village in Guinea-Bissau to find work as a servant in the capital after a magic man declares she is cursed. Living amongst colonists and later, as the spurned wife of a village chief who wants to "expel the whites", she eventually finds love with a local schoolteacher. The plot centres on Ndani's coming-of-age in multiple environs of subjugation. Mindful of the oral tradition that shapes his prose, Silá evokes the creole language and its strained relationship with Portuguese, which is facilitated by the translator Jethro Soutar's dedication to maintaining context and sentiment. This bittersweet novel offers a snapshot of a country whose history is little known outside its own borders.'

M.Rene Bradshaw in *The Times Literary Supplement*

'Silá delights in using humour to spear hypocrisy and there is some startling imagery at play in many passages. He also demonstrates a flair for technically adventurous storytelling, with the novel featuring one-sided conversations here and deft uses of repetition there. The passages in which Ndani falls in love at last are beautiful and joyous, as are the descriptions of her discovery of sexual fulfilment.'

Ann Morgan Book of the Month in *A Year of Reading the World*

'It's the first novel by an author from Guinea-Bissau to be translated into English. Books like these are important. They change the way we think and talk about African fiction. They refine our taste for African writing. The more we are exposed to different forms of African storytelling the more we appreciate the diversity in African literary forms. It tells the story of an ill-fated girl named Ndani. After a medicine man reveals that her future will be a string of disasters, she tries to change the course of her life by moving to the city. But of course, you already know that her attempt to escape her tragic fate will be way more complicated than she imagined. Intriguing plot! Congrats to Silá and Dedalus Books for gifting the world of Anglophone literature with such a beautiful book.'

Ainehi Edoro in *Brittle Papers*

'*The Ultimate Tragedy* by Abdulai Silá is the first novel from Guinea-Bissau to be translated into English. Its publication in an excellent translation by Jethro Soutar is therefore something of a cultural event. It is the affecting and vivid story of Ndani, who leaves her village to work as a maid for a Portuguese family in the city. Expelled after refusing the master's advances, she starts to drift, then marries a village chief. Cultural differences take hold against a tumultuous political background.'

Thomas Tallon in *The Tablet*

£9.99   ISBN 978 1 910213 54 4   187p   B. Format